Consuela Travis and the Domino Effect

Barbara Kaster

Copyright 2007 Barbara Kaster
All Rights Reserved

ISBN: 978-1-4303-1781-4

Contents

Chapter One: The Set-Up 1

Chapter Two: The Search 29

Chapter Three: The Domino Effect 67

Chapter Four: Final Answers 81

Chapter Five: The Deposition 105

Chapter Six: A New Beginning 135

Chapter One
The Set-Up

The rain began just as the horse came around the pick-up. Joe Baxter dismounted and flipped the reins over the horse's head and lead him into the barn. There was a sudden clap of thunder and the horse spooked, crabbing sideways.

"Easy fella. Easy," Joe said keeping his voice steady. The horse remained tense but stopped jerking on the reins. Joe opened the stall and lead him in. He held the reins in his left hand as he undid the cinch and slipped the saddle off. He steadied the saddle on his leg and then flipped it up on the railing.

"OK? Good boy. Take it easy. Smell how fresh the air is? That's what lightening does, so don't get all spooked," said Joe laughing to himself for explaining physics to a horse. He slid the halter over the horse's head and gave him a pat on the neck. Joe heard the rain begin to really pound on the barn roof. Although he had grown up in West Texas, he was amazed at how quickly a storm could blow up out of what had been a cloudless sky until an hour ago.

He stood in the barn door, hesitated, then ducked his head and rushed toward the house, his boots splashing in puddles which had already formed.

His wife Margaret watched him from the kitchen window. She was relieved he had gotten back. A man on a horse is an easy target for lightening.

He burst through the door and stood on the back porch, dripping wet. Margaret opened the door to the kitchen, offered him a towel and said, "Hey cowboy, can you use this?"

Joe grinned and took the towel. They walked into the kitchen and Margaret poured him a cup of coffee as he sat and rubbed the towel on his face and neck. She turned on the overhead light. The sky had gotten dark as the rain continued to pour down in great sheets swept by the wind.

She sat down by Joe and finished her coffee. They had been married for eight years, a marriage not without its problems. Money had been tight and still was, but she was proud of Joe and the fact that they now owned the mortgage to 300 acres of land, the house and barn. They raised some cattle and had 200 acres in cotton and, so far, they had been able to meet all the payments.

"Damn," said Joe looking outside. "I wish I didn't have to go to town in the mess."

"Can't you wait awhile and see if it stops raining?"

"Nah, I promised Dave I'd meet him at two. You know how he gets. The picnic is just a month away and he's determined to make this the biggest Aggie picnic ever. Did I tell you he wants to do a rodeo with the picnic?"

Margaret laughed, "Rodeo, my foot! When you get together all you do is drink beer and sing the Aggie War Hymn!"

Joe laughed and went upstairs to change clothes. Margaret picked up her cup of coffee and stood looking out the kitchen window. She could barely see the barn there was so much rain, but she could see several cows and their calves huddle under a large cottonwood tree.

Joe walked back into the kitchen, leaned down and kissed Margaret on the cheek. "OK Maggie-pants, hold down the fort. I'll be back by six."

"Joe, be careful. The road will be awful," Margaret said as she walked to the back door with him. He took a yellow slicker off the peg by the door, put it on and ran to the truck.

He started the engine and turned the knob for the windshield wipers. He checked to make sure they were on high because they were clattering back and forth but seemed to have little effect. Joe turned on the radio which had lots of static but he laughed as he heard Willie Nelson singing "Blue Eyes Crying in the Rain."

Joe drove out the long dirt road to the highway. He had turned on his headlights and he strained to see if any cars were coming. He didn't see anything and stepped on the accelerator. The truck slid slightly but he quickly regained control.

Five miles out of El Paso he began to relax as the rain slackened and he could see Mt Franklin. He saw a billboard advertising Maya de Mexico in Juarez and remembered the first time he and Margaret had gone to the store and had watched the glassblowers and the kids who made colorful paper flowers. He and Margaret had considered buying some of the handsome hand made Mexican furniture but Joe couldn't get Margaret to say whether she really wanted the furniture or not. She had a tendency to agree with whatever he thought.

CHAPTER ONE

Joe thought about the tractor he was considering buying. He wanted the new John Deere, but the thing was damned expensive. Margaret wouldn't say whether she thought they should buy it or not. It wasn't that Joe minded making the decisions, but he wanted to look at the marriage as a partnership. He tried to take Margaret's feelings into consideration. She was getting better about saying what she thought, but he wanted her to be more assertive about her feelings.

When they had been in high school he rather liked the way she adored him and always agreed with whatever he said. During the last few years, really since they had been married, his love for her had deepened. He realized he loved her for herself and not just because she loved him.

Suddenly Joe laughed out loud and a sheepish grin spread across his face. Sure, he thought. Sure you want her to be herself, to be assertive! He remembered that only last week Margaret had told him she wanted to cut her hair. He had been appalled at the idea and had told her so. He had always loved her long, rich brown hair. He did his best to change her mind and he had succeeded. He felt foolish now, thinking about it. By God, he thought, I'll tell her tonight to cut her hair.

He saw the car coming toward him but didn't pay any particular attention. Suddenly, the car veered into his path. He jerked the wheel to the right but knew it wouldn't help.

The car hit his left front fender. There was a terrifying crunch and the sound of metal tearing. He heard glass breaking as his head hit the windshield.

Joe was dazed. He felt rain on his neck but he couldn't move. It hurt to breath. His thoughts were jumbled. He was draped over the steering wheel. The horn was blaring. It wouldn't stop. He passed out.

Somebody was talking but Joe couldn't open his eyes. He felt hands on his shoulders. When they lifted him out of the truck he heard someone scream. He realized it was him. God, his leg hurt. Sweet Jesus, what happened?

A young man found the wreck. He thought the man in the car was dead and that the guy in the truck might be about to die. He used his cell phone to call the sheriff.

The Medivac unit and the deputy sheriff arrived at the wreck at the same time. Joe was unconscious and was pinned in the wreckage. The sheriff had used a crowbar to pry open the smashed door.

"Let's be real careful, Sheriff," said the paramedic. "He's got a nasty cut on his forehead. His seatbelt kept him from going through the window, but I guess it came unhinged and he banged his head real hard. Too bad this old truck didn't have air bags."

The paramedic slipped a soft cervical collar around Joe's neck. His leg was pinned by the motor and they managed to shift it enough to free his leg and lift him out of the truck. Joe screamed when they moved him. They got him on the stretcher and loaded into the Medivac unit.

The driver radioed ahead to the hospital, "This is Medivac Unit 1. We are transporting the patient. His ID says he is Joe Baxter and he is 33 years old. He has multiple injuries. His BP is 130 over 80, pulse is 100 and thready. He is barely conscious. His pupils are equal and reactive. He appears to have chest trauma and a broken left leg. He has multiple facial lacerations. We estimate arrival in ten minutes."

Joe opened his eyes. He looked at the paramedic and whispered, "What happened?"

"You've been in a wreck. We're taking you to the hospital."

Joe began to struggle. "I can't breathe. Help me. I can't breathe."

The paramedic reached over for the oxygen mask and placed it over Joe's nose and mouth. Joe continued to struggle.

When the ambulance arrived at the hospital the paramedics rushed Joe into the emergency room. An intern was waiting and immediately lead them to the trauma room.

The intern, Paul Edwards, quickly examined Joe. He could hear liquid in Joe's lungs and the abdomen was tight, a sign of internal bleeding. The left leg was obviously broken. Paul guessed the left foot was smashed from the look of the boot.

"Karen," Paul said as he continued to evaluate Joe's injuries, "You're going to have to get someone from surgery and someone from orthopedics to the operating room. This guy's gotta have surgery right away. Get X-ray down here stat. We need pictures of the left leg, the abdomen and chest and cervical spine. I'll get IV lines started. Get on the phone."

Karen Welch turned to the phone on the wall. She knew as she dialed that it was going to be tough to get an operating room staff. It was Friday afternoon and the senior staff would be leaving for the weekend. This patient was going to require more than the skill of interns.

She managed to catch Sam Boswell, the chief of surgery, just as he was leaving for a golf game. He reluctantly agreed to prepare to operate.

Don Roberts, one of the best orthopedic surgeons in El Paso was just finishing an operation and agreed to look at Joe when they sent him up.

Karen looked at the card they had taken from Joe's wallet. It showed his address as San Elizario, a small farming community thirty miles from El Paso. She found the telephone number and dialed. When Margaret answered, Karen told her Joe had been in a wreck and that he was at Memorial Hospital.

When Sam Boswell walked into the operating room he saw the chief surgical resident, Randy Patterson, looking at a set of X-rays on the lighted box.

He walked over and glanced at the film.

"What have we got, Randy?"

"Hard to tell with these damn X-rays. I'll leave it to the orthopods to figure these out. But I do know we've got a guy who got the hell smashed out of himself in a wreck. I'm sure there is lots of bleeding in the chest and stomach. They inserted a chest tube downstairs and it's draining fresh blood. I just did a tap of the peritoneum and we've got fresh blood there too. He's got bleeders and we'll have to go in and find them."

"OK," said Sam. "When will the orthopods get here?"

Randy shrugged his shoulders and said, "I'm not sure. Roberts is finishing something in OR 3 and then he'll be here."

"Well, let's get started. This guy's got internal bleeding and we can't wait. You open and I'll supervise."

Randy nodded at Sam. He needed all the surgery he could get. He would finish his residency in six months and he still felt he needed more experience. He looked over at the table and saw that Joe was anesthetized and they could get started.

Randy began the exploratory laparotomy and soon discovered the blood in the peritoneum and several lacerations of the caudate lobe of the liver. The bleeding sites were tied off and controlled. Randy irrigated the abdomen. He was about to start closing the incision when Sam leaned over and said, "How many gastrostomies have you done?"

Randy looked at Sam. He was surprised by the suggestion that they do a gastrostomy, a procedure that would allow feeding directly into the stomach. He recognized there were pulmonary problems which might require a tube down the windpipe. Randy knew that the tube, if they had to place one, would make eating impossible but he would have waited to do the gastrostomy until it was clear they were going to have to place the windpipe tube. Even then, he would probably have opted for IV feeding for the short time it would be likely they would have the tube down the windpipe. He hesitated.

"Come on boy. You've got to learn to do gastrostomies. I'm late for golf."

Randy was in no mood to argue with the chief of surgery. He began the gastrostomy.

"You're doing fine, Randy. I'm going to run now. Follow this guy until he leaves the recovery room. Dr. Phillips will cover my patients this weekend. Just report to him." Sam backed away from the table.

Don Roberts and his assistant, Paul Morales, had entered the OR during the laparotomy and were standing by the lighted X-ray box. They nodded to Sam Boswell as he left.

They saw from the X-rays that Joe's left foot was broken in several places and that he had fractured his left tibia. They noted three rib fractures on his left side.

"Damn, look at this!" said Paul, indicating the X-ray of the cervical spine. Don moved to Paul's side and stared at the film. The X-ray showed the first five cervical bones.

"Why didn't they get pictures down to C-7. They know we've got to see down to C-7!" muttered Paul.

"Rushed I guess and this guy's got big shoulders. You know how hard that makes it to see down to C-7. Well, at least he's clean to C-5. We'll get better pictures later. Let's get started on that leg."

Don and Paul walked to the table to see what progress the surgeons were making. Randy was finishing the gastrostomy. When the incision was closed and the G-tube anchored, Randy looked up and said, "All yours."

Don and Paul began to work. They inserted a pin in the tibia to hold the fracture closed and began to repair the foot. The foot looked pretty hopeless. It had been mangled by the motor as it crashed through the firewall of the truck. They did what they could and put a cast on the foot and leg.

"You need to do anything about this guy's head injury?" asked the anesthesiologist.

"Nah, the skull X-rays looked OK," answered Don.

"He has a nasty gash on his forehead," the anesthesiologist pointed out.

Chapter One

"It's been sutured hasn't it?"
"Yea."
"Let's let it go at that."

When Margaret got to the hospital Joe was still in surgery. She was taken to the surgical waiting room and given a cup of coffee. When she tried to drink it her hands shook and she spilled some.

She tried to calm down. She had left the house in such a hurry that she hadn't called anyone. She put the coffee down and looked around for a phone. She saw one on the wall, stood and started to walk toward it.

"Margaret?" she heard someone ask tentatively. She looked around and saw an attractive woman sitting on the couch. It took her a minute to recognize Consuela Travis.

"Connie?" she inquired.

Consuela stood and reached for Margaret's hand. She could see the worried look on her face. "Margaret, what are you doing here? What's wrong?" asked Consuela as she firmly gripped Margaret's hand.

"It's Joe. He was in a wreck. They're operating now," said Margaret, tears streaming down her face. "What are you doing here?"

"They're doing some minor surgery on my dad. God, I'm sorry to hear about Joe. Can I do anything to help? Is he OK?"

"I don't know. I haven't talked to the doctors. They called and said he was in a wreck and that he was at Memorial. I'm going to call our parents now. I'll talk to you in a few minutes."

Consuela sat down and watched Margaret as she went to the phone. She hadn't seen Margaret Baxter in years. They had gone to high school together at the Radford School. Consuela remembered the shy girl when she first enrolled at Radford. Margaret had grown up in Marfa where her parents had a ranch. Her mother had decided to send her to school in El Paso for two reasons: to get a better education and because she thought Margaret and Joe Baxter were far too serious about each other for their age.

Consuela and Margaret had moved in different social circles at school. Consuela had been at Radford since the first grade and she was a natural leader. In addition, she was the only child of William Randolf Travis, a wealthy and powerful rancher and attorney. On the other hand, Margaret was shy and her parents had made a great sacrifice to send her to Radford. Paying her tuition, room and board had cost them all their savings. Nevertheless, by the time they graduated Margaret and Consuela were friends but they had seen little of each other in the past few years.

Consuela glanced at her watch and saw her father had been in surgery for an hour. She glanced up and smiled as she saw her mother come back into the waiting room. Maria Travis was a handsome, tall woman. She had jet black eyes and her black hair was still lush but now flecked with grey.

"Any word?" asked Maria.

"No. We should hear something in a few minutes. Mama, see that woman on the phone. That's Margaret Baxter. Remember her from Radford?"

Maria glanced at Margaret. "Yes, that's Margaret Simpson. I remember that she finally did marry that nice Joe Baxter. What's the matter? She's crying."

"Joe was in a wreck. She's calling their parents."

"Aye, Madre de Dios...he was such a nice boy."

Consuela nodded in agreement. Joe was a nice guy. She remembered the proud look on Margaret's face when Joe would come to Radford for the dances. He was handsome in a rugged way. Consuela remembered he was always gentle and sweet. Joe had gone to A&M at the same time she had gone to the University of Texas. She saw him at a couple of football games.

Consuela looked at her watch again. She was beginning to get anxious about her father. Bill Travis was the most independent and tough man she had ever known. She adored him. His parents had been killed when he was fifteen and since then he had done pretty much as he pleased. He was a descendent of William B. Travis who died at the Alamo and of William Randolph of Virginia. He took after the Texan. He had gone to the University of Texas Law School, graduating as Notes Editor of the Texas Law Review. He returned to El Paso to establish a law practice and to oversee the operation of the Travis ranch.

When he was thirty he had caused a social scandal by marrying Maria Frenandez, the daughter of the ranch foreman. Maria lacked the sophistication of Bill's friends, the sophistication learned by years of money and travel. And she was Mexican. But she had what Bill admired: gentleness and a luminous beauty. She also loved the ranch as much as he did. They had weathered the social storm by simply ignoring it. As the years passed, people learned to accept Maria for her good sense and quiet pride in her own heritage.

Chapter One

The first time Maria had shown up at a great social gathering in her Mexican mantilla, a beautiful embroidered shawl, there had been snickers. Now the mantillas and some beautiful Mexican jewelry she often wore on special occasions were expected. When Maria refused the invitation to join the Junior League, preferring instead to continue her work with poor Mexicans in the barrios, the social leaders were shocked, determined to ignore Maria Travis from then on. But when it became clear that it was Maria who was doing the ignoring, they were flabbergasted. Maria was simply too busy and devoted to the causes she cared about. Finally, they accepted Maria.

By the time Consuela was born, the Travis family was powerful, if still viewed as different. The Travis' didn't notice. Consuela always moved easily between the Mexican world of her mother and the rich Anglo world of her father. When she went to the University of Texas, no one was surprised. The children of the Texas power elite had most often gone to Texas. But when she was accepted at Harvard Law School and decided instead to go to the University of Texas Law School as her father had done, a few were surprised. When she too graduated as Notes Editor of the Texas Law Review people began to realize they had a female Bill Travis on their hands.

Consuela had joined her father in the practice of law and now Travis and Travis was a firm to be reckoned with. Bill had never been particularly serious about practicing law, much preferring to run the ranch. At first, other lawyers thought Consuela might be as casual about the law as her father. Bill Travis was a first rate attorney when he accepted a case, but that wasn't very often. They learned that Consuela was also a first rate attorney and that she was damn serious about the law. She was also a genius for winning cases for poor Mexicans, much to the chagrin of those representing the wealthy who lost the cases.

Margaret walked back from the phone and both Maria and Consuela stood.

"Margarita, I'm so sorry about Joe. What can we do to help you?" said Maria as she put her arms around Margaret.

"Thank you, Mrs. Travis. I don't know what I am going to do. I've called our parents and they are on the way."

"Margaret, do you want me to go see if I can find out anything about Joe?" offered Consuela.

"Oh, Connie...would you? I'm so worried."

Consuela smiled and said, "I'll be back in a minute."

Margaret watched Consuela walk out of the waiting room. She had always admired the way Consuela took charge, the way she never seemed to be afraid of anyone. Joe. What was happening to Joe. Consuela would find out.

That evening Joe was moved from the recovery room to the ICU. He had regained consciousness in the recovery room but he was kept heavily sedated because the endotracheal tube was still in place to assist his breathing.

Margaret was allowed to see him for a few minutes. She was shocked because he looked so pale and sick. His left leg was in a cast. All the intravenous tubes and the monitoring equipment terrified her but she tried not to show her fear.

"Joe, can you hear me?" she asked as she leaned over the bed. She stroked his forehead and stared at him, praying that he would wake up. His eyelids fluttered and he opened his eyes and looked at her. He seemed to see her and then he closed his eyes.

"Sweetheart, you're going to be OK. You were in a wreck but you're going to be fine. Can you hear me?"

Joe remained still and all Margaret could hear was the sound of the breathing machine pumping air in and out. There was something awful about the unceasing regularity of the machine, something inhuman. She kissed Joe's cheek and patted his hand.

A nurse came in and said, "I'm sorry Mrs. Baxter, but you'll have to leave now. You can come back in an hour. Mr. Baxter is heavily sedated and we must let him rest."

Margaret kissed Joe again and, with tears streaming down her cheeks, she left the room. She walked to the central nurses station and stood there wanting to talk to someone. No one paid any attention to her. Finally Margaret walked over to a nurse who was writing in a chart and said, "Excuse me, can you help me for a minute?"

The nurse looked up and smiled. "Of course. What can I do for you?"

"I'm Mrs. Baxter. My husband is in that room," Margaret said as she pointed to Joe's room. "I wonder if I'm going to get to talk to the doctor?"

"The doctor hasn't talked to you yet?"

"No, and I want to know how my husband is."

"Mrs. Baxter, I'm sure the doctor will be here shortly. Why don't you go over there and wait. I'll let you know as soon as he comes."

CHAPTER ONE

"Could you please tell me the doctor's name."

"Let me see. Baxter? Ah, that would be Dr. Boswell. I'll watch for him."

"Thank you."

Fifteen minutes later a young man walked over to Margaret, reached down to shake her hand and said, "Hi. I'm Dr. Patterson, your husband's doctor."

Margaret was slightly confused because she had been expecting a Dr. Boswell, but she was so relieved to finally talk to a doctor that she ignored her confusion. She was surprised, however, at the youth of the doctor.

"How is Joe?"

"His condition is stable right now, but he has suffered many serious injuries."

"Is he going to be alright?"

"Frankly, it's too soon to tell. He had some internal bleeding but I think we've stopped that. He has lots of cuts and bruises and several broken bones. I've just talked to the orthopedic surgeons and they are worried about his left foot. It is really smashed and they will do some more X-rays tomorrow, but it looks bad."

"What does that mean?"

"Well, they will have to monitor it carefully."

"But will it be alright?"

"I don't know, Mrs. Baxter. Your husband suffered some very serious injuries and we'll watch him carefully," Randy said smiling, trying to give her some encouragement.

After the doctor left, Margaret sat quietly. She looked at her watch and saw that it was eight o'clock. She was relieved because that meant that their parents should be arriving any minute. She wanted someone to be with her because she was frightened. Joe looked awful. Connie had been there until seven o'clock. Mr. Travis was down on the surgical floor and Connie said he was doing fine. Connie had sat with her for awhile, but Margaret, afraid she was imposing on her friend, had assured her she was fine.

All she could do now was wait.

The next morning the endotracheal tube was removed and Joe was placed on a respirator when he showed signs of difficulty in breathing.

One member of his family was allowed to see him for a few minutes each hour and Margaret and Joe's parents rotated turns.

Joe was conscious most of the time and seemed frightened by his difficulty in breathing. He also complained that his left leg felt numb. Orelia Ortiz, his primary care nurse on the morning shift, tried to reassure him.

"Joe, take it easy. You're OK. This machine is breathing for you. Quit struggling. Try to relax. I know this is uncomfortable, but you're getting better," she said as she checked the oxygen flow and the intravenous tubes. She bent down to check the urine flow from the catheter tube. The bag showed a slight increase in urine output over the previous hour. That, at least, was a good sign.

Randy Patterson walked in and stood for a few minutes looking at Joe's chart. He saw that Joe's temperature was slightly elevated but that generally his vital signs were stable. Randy nodded at Orelia and moved to the side of the bed. Joe seemed to have dozed off.

"He is still frightened by his breathing difficulty," began Ofelia. "He has also been complaining that his left leg is numb. His grasp is weak bilaterally. His fluid balance is good."

"OK," acknowledged Randy. He pulled the sheet off Joe and began his examination. He saw that bruises were developing on Joe's chest and on his forehead. He changed the dressing on the abdominal incision and checked the G-tube.

"Listen, Orelia, he seems to be doing fine. I don't know about the numbness but that's the orthopedics department's problem. Tell them. Meanwhile, I'll leave orders for some lab work that I want done today. We'll get some blood counts, some blood gas studies...the whole range of stuff. I'll leave the pain meds note. Let's keep infusing the morphine in the IV line. Tomorrow we can start weaning him from the respirator."

Orelia made notes on the pad she carried and nodded to Randy. She was worried about the numbness and glad that orthopedics rounds were scheduled in a few minutes.

"Is his wife in the waiting room?" Randy asked.

"Last time I looked she was. Their parents are here too."

"OK, I'll go talk to them."

Randy walked to the waiting room and saw Margaret. He smiled at her, walked over and sat next to her. She quickly introduced him to Joe's parents and to hers.

"How's Joe?" asked Mr. Baxter.

Chapter One

"I'm happy to say he seems much better today. His signs are stable. He's damned uncomfortable, obviously, but he seems to be recovering from the surgery."

"He's going to be OK then?" asked Margaret anxiously.

"He's not out of the woods yet, Mrs. Baxter, but I'm hopeful."

Margaret smiled slightly. For the first time she felt some hope. Joe looked so pale and seemed so disoriented. Margaret was happy to rely on the doctor's judgement that Joe was getting better.

"What about his foot?" asked Joe's mother. "Margaret told us it was smashed. Is it going to be alright?"

"Uh, actually, that's hard to say. As you know the whole left leg and foot are in a cast. I did check his toes and they seem OK. That's really the business of the orthopedic surgeons. You need to talk to them. They'll be around soon."

On Monday morning, as Consuela was almost finished writing her notes so she could ask pertinent questions for the deposition she was taking that afternoon, the phone rang. She picked up the receiver and cradled it between her shoulder and ear as she finished writing.

"Yes," she said.

"It's Fred. Want to talk to him now?" asked her secretary, Marge Kern.

"OK. Thanks," she said as she put the pen down and reached over and punched a lighted button on the phone. "Hi! What are you up to?"

"Hi, Consuela. Just wanted to tell you I glanced in on your dad this morning and the old tiger is complaining and grousing and wants the hell out of the hospital. In other words, he's back to normal," laughed Fred.

Consuela laughed and said, "Glad to hear it. He was asleep early this morning when I went by. I'm going back at noon to see him. Thanks for checking up on him."

"I'm going to be at the hospital the rest of the morning. I've got five or six patients to check and some notes to dictate. Want to have lunch after you see your dad?"

"Sure. I'll come by the doctor's lounge, OK?"

"Terrific. See you soon."

Consuela hung up the phone and smiled. She had dated Fred Cunningham for years. They had met at the University and had dated frequently while they were undergraduates. She had fond memories of afternoons on Lake Travis (named, she was proud to acknowledge, for her ancestor, William B. Travis), memories of days spent at Barton Springs during final exam week when they would both sit on the grassy bank of the pool cramming for final exams and taking fast plunges into the frigid waters when the sun got too hot. They had done the trip to Dallas for the Texas-Oklahoma football game, standing in front of the Adolphus Hotel at midnight with thousands of people drinking beer to excess and singing "The Eyes of Texas", trying to drown out those singing "Boomer Sooner."

Fred had gone to Galveston to medical school while Consuela stayed in Austin in law school. They were both so busy that they had seen little of each other, but had talked on the phone frequently. Both had dated other people but their relationship had endured.

Fred had done a surgical residency with Denton Cooley in Houston and had accepted a position with a group of heart surgeons in El Paso, influenced in part because Consuela was in El Paso. During the past few months Fred had begun to think seriously about marriage.

Consuela gathered up her notes and put them in her briefcase. She was looking forward to lunch with Fred. As she started out the door, she remembered Margaret Baxter. She'd check on Joe and Margaret too.

Orelia found Paul Morales reading charts at the nurse's station. He was late for rounds and she was glad to see him.

"Hi, Dr. Morales," she said as she walked up to the counter.

"Oh, Orelia. Hi. Sorry I'm late. They had me hopping in the clinic all morning."

"I understand, but I'm glad you're here. Joe Baxter is really agitated. The nurse's reports from yesterday afternoon and last night indicate that he really began to be agitated late Sunday. He keeps complaining about numbness in his left leg."

"Not surprising. He smashed the hell out of that leg."

"I know, but when I test his reflexes he shows very little hand strength."

"Oh?"

"Yes. It's in the Nurse's Progress Report," said Orelia. She was annoyed because it was obvious Paul had not read the Nurse's Progress report. Typical doctor. Doctor's only read other doctor's reports. Never what the nurse's wrote. Orelia appreciated the year's of training the doctors had, but nurses had training too and were with the patient day and night. The doctors buzzed in and out and saw the patient about five minutes a day.

"Well, let's go look."

Paul and Orelia walked down to Joe's room. They saw that Joe looked uncomfortable and perhaps frightened. Paul went to the bed and tried to shake Joe's hand.

"Hi, Mr. Baxter. I'm Dr. Morales, one of your doctors. Do you remember me? You've been pretty sleepy all weekend when I've checked you. I'll be taking care of your orthopedic problems," said Paul as he squeezed Joe's hand. There was little response.

Paul began to examine Joe's leg. The toes on the left side felt a little cool. That worried Paul because it meant that the blood circulation to the foot was impaired. Still, there was circulation and when the swelling reduced the circulation would improve. Paul tested Joe's reflexes and found adequate lower extremity response, but he did find the hand grasp to be weak on both sides.

He chatted with Joe briefly and then nodded to Orelia. When they got to the hallway Paul said, "I don't know. The hand grasp is weak. But he suffered a hell of a trauma. I don't think there is anything to worry about. I am worried about that foot. The circulation isn't terrific. We've really got to watch that. I've checked Dr. Patterson's orders and they look fine to me. We don't need to add anything. Call me if there is any change."

Orelia nodded. Maybe the doctors were right. But she was uneasy about all the complaints of numbness and the weak hand grasp. Sounded like a spinal cord injury. Still, she knew Joe had X-rays when he was admitted. If he had a spinal cord injury they would have spotted it. Perhaps it was just swelling around the spinal cord.

Orelia went back to Joe's room. She got a wash cloth and washed his face with cool water. "Joe," she said, "I'm going to give you a Tylenol suppository. That will bring your temperature down and make you more comfortable. OK?"

Joe turned his face slightly toward her and nodded. "Yes," he whispered. "Is my wife here?"

"Yes. I'll let her come in a few minutes."

"Good," whispered Joe.

When Margaret came in she was relieved to see Joe awake. She rushed to the bed and kissed him.

"Hi," Joe whispered and tried to smile.

"Sweetheart, how do you feel?"

"Awful."

"I know, but the doctor says you're getting better."

Joe nodded at Margaret and then closed his eyes. She stood for a moment holding his hand.

When she went back to the waiting room she was relieved to be able to tell their parents that Joe had been able to talk and that he did seem better. After a few minutes of talking quietly in the waiting room, they all decided to go to the hospital cafeteria and eat.

As they were eating, her father said, "Margaret honey, your mother and I are going back to San Elizario this afternoon. Somebody has got to take care of the cattle and look after the place. We fed them yesterday but we'll just go back this afternoon and stay there until you can come home. Your big dog, Barton, doesn't like to be alone either. The Baxters will stay here with you and Joe."

"Oh my God! I'd totally forgotten about the animals. Thank you Daddy. And Mom, give Barton a big hug for Joe. That dog won't understand where Joe is. He'll be lost."

Her mother smiled and nodded. "I will and you tell Joe we're at the farm and not to worry about anything."

Suddenly, a worried look crossed Margaret's face and she said, "What about things in Marfa? Who's looking after everything on both the ranches?"

Mrs. Baxter reached out her hand and patted Margaret. "Child, don't worry. The boys are there and they're taking care of everything."

Just then Consuela Travis walked up. Margaret stood and smiled broadly and said, "Oh Connie! Joe is better. He could talk to me this morning."

"I'm delighted to hear it!"

Consuela said hello to the Baxters and Simpsons. Then she introduced Dr. Fred Cunningham to them. Margaret was impressed. He was very tall and handsome. He had sandy colored hair and a warm smile.

Consuela and Fred returned to their table and finished their lunch. They agreed to have dinner together and Consuela left to go see her father who had been asleep when she first arrived. She wanted to talk to him before she took the deposition that afternoon. The case involved some people he knew and she wanted his advice.

Consuela stood in the doorway of her father's hospital room. Maria was sitting in a chair by the bed reading the El Paso Times. Bill, with his half-glasses perched on his nose, was frowning at some book. Consuela smiled and watched them. She had seen them like this so many times, both reading quietly. Only when she was older had she realized how unusual it was for two people to be able to read quietly together. They might sit for hours together this way, the silence broken occasionally when one of them would read something out loud to the other.

Bill glanced up, sensing someone looking at him. His face became radiant when he saw it was Consuela. "Hey, baby girl!" he roared.

Consuela laughed and walked into the room. She grinned at her mother and gave her father a big hug and a kiss. "How do you feel?" she inquired.

"I'll feel better when they let me out of this prison," replied her father, laughing.

"He's fine. The doctor said he could go home this afternoon," said Maria, smiling.

"That's terrific! I came by earlier but you were snoozing," said Consulea as she pulled up a chair.

"Fred came by this morning. He said he looked at my charts and I'm going to survive," said Bill, grinning.

"Consuela, you tell him we appreciate it," said Maria. "How is Joe Baxter doing? Do you know?"

"He is doing better. We saw Margaret and their parents in the cafeteria."

"Oh, I'm glad. Gracias a Dios," said Maria, instinctively crossing herself. "By the way, I think I'll ask Fred to come out to the ranch next weekend, OK?"

"Of course, I'd love it. When are you going to the ranch? Don't you think you should stay in town a few days?"

"We'll stay up the valley until Wednesday and then go to the ranch. I've got a bunch of mother cows ready to deliver," said Bill.

"And you've got to help them deliver," laughed Consuela.

"Damn right!"

The Travis' had a beautiful Spanish style home in the upper valley of El Paso. The house was made of baked adobe bricks and had enclosed patios, Spanish tile floors and was surrounded by pecan and cottonwood trees. Bill and Maria spent about half their time at the house, but as much as they loved the house, they were happiest at the ranch.

"Hey, Pop. I want to talk to you about the Gonzales case. I'm going to talk to Dolores Gonzales this afternoon," said Consuela.

"Fire away," said Bill. He took off his glasses and gave Consuela his absolute attention.

"As you remember, Dolores Gonzales and her little girl, Julia, were crossing Copia at that light by the Oasis Restaurant. Jack Porter ran the red light and hit Julia. The cops gave him a ticket and he entered a nolo plea. We filed suit. Well, yesterday, Mark Harper, who's representing Porter, called and offered a settlement."

"What did they offer?"

"To pay all the medical expenses, which are considerable, and a cash settlement of $10,000. He made it clear that was going to be their only offer."

"What did you say?"

"I said I'd talk to Mrs. Gonzales today and get back to him. I've got to take a deposition on the Norton case and then I'm going to see her about four this afternoon. I really don't know how to advise her. They need the money, no doubt about that. But I really do believe if we went to trial I could win her a lot more."

"Ah, the eternal cry of the attorney," laughed Bill.

Consuela laughed too but continued, "The thing is Dad, not only did Julia suffer a broken leg but she's got a hell of a scar now on the leg. She won't wear shorts anymore. She won't go swimming. And Dolores was so traumatized by seeing her child get hit by a car that she's had continuing nightmares since then. She probably ought to be in therapy but can't afford it. She can't work full time. I think we can also collect on Julia's behalf for the loss of her mother's ability to care for her."

"Consuela, sweetheart, you certainly might win if you go to trial. You might lose. How long before a trial? Porter's lawyers can get the trial postponed at least once, probably a couple of times. How would the Gonzales family survive in the interim? Maybe the settlement would be in their best interests."

"But Bill," said Maria who had been quietly listening, "they have suffered an awful thing. If Consuela can win a big settlement for them, she should."

"Maria, mi corazon, our daughter might lose the case. Probably not, but then what? The bigger problem is that it might be more than a year before it even went to trial. How can the Gonzales family survive. They can't pay their bills now."

"Consuela would win" said Maria firmly.

Both Bill and Consuela laughed. Consuela looked at her mother and said, "I would win for sure if you were on the jury. But Dad is right. It would be profoundly difficult for them to wait that long. It might be as long as two years before we went to trial. The court system is jammed."

Bill said, "And another thing, Consuela. If you went to trail on this thing, it would take a hell of a lot of time. What about your other clients? Can they afford for you to take the time worrying this thing to trail?"

"It would be hard, but I've looked at it and I believe I can do it and still attend to the other cases."

"Bill, do you really think she should advise them to take the settlement?" asked Maria.

"Hell no! Consuela should be realistic with them. Tell them all the facts about life at trials. Explain how long they'd have to wait. Explain that she could lose, although she thinks they'd win considerably more money. But the decision must be theirs."

"You're right Dad. But, do you think I'd win if we went to trail?"

"Hell yes! That Jack Porter somehow avoided a sobriety test that day. Bet you could do a little work and find out he had been drinking that day. I know the guy. He drinks."

"I agree. However, I don't know if the Gonzales' can wait for a trial. They need the money now, which Porter's lawyer certainly understands."

Consuela stood and kissed her parents. "I'm off to fight for Truth and Justice!" she said laughing. "I'll drive up the valley to see you two tonight. Maybe I'll bring Fred. We're having dinner about six."

"Do bring him! We'll see you later."

"Cuidado, chica," said Maria.

The night nurse checked on Joe at midnight. He was log-rolled to change his position, a maneuver that caused him only mild discomfort. His grasp was still weak bilaterally, but he could hold both arms up. His right leg seemed reasonably strong and he could move his right toes. The toes on his left foot remained cool.

Joe was belching, a sign that the G-tube needed irrigating and the intern on night call was called. He irrigated the tube and Joe seemed more comfortable. The nurse wondered why the hell the G-tube was still in place.

By the next morning, Joe was much more alert but agitated. Orelia checked on him and was pleased, although he was still complaining about numbness. She checked his medication orders and saw he was still getting morphine. There was a standing order for Valium if his agitation increased. Orelia decided to give him the Valium and he soon calmed down.

Both Dr. Roberts and Dr. Morales came by for orthopedic rounds. Orelia was glad to see them both. She liked Paul Morales and thought he was good but his lack of experience worried her in this case. She was still worried about the numbness.

The doctors also found weak bilateral hand grasp, but it was clear to Orelia they were much more interested in the problems with the left foot.

As they left the room Orelia said, "I hate to harp on anything, but what about the weak bilateral hand grasp?"

Roberts, who was generally good natured, seemed a bit irritated but smiled and said, "Paul, make the woman happy. Let's put a soft cervical collar around the boy's neck."

Paul smiled and nodded. Orelia was relieved and went to the supply room to get the soft collar. Paul and Don continued down the hallway to the chart rack.

"Maybe we ought to get another X-ray of the cervical spine. What do you think?" asked Paul.

"Why? The one's taken at admission were clear, weren't they?"

"They were clear to C-5. Remember, they didn't show down to C-7."

"Damn, that's right. Hell, I guess it wouldn't hurt. See if you can schedule him for X-ray this morning. While they're at it, lets get another series on the left foot and leg."

Paul made the arrangements and Joe was taken to the radiology department at noon. That afternoon, Paul, Don and Simon Webster, the head of radiology, met to examine the X-rays. They sat at a table that faced the long, lighted X-ray reading box. Joe's latest X-rays were clipped to the top of the box and the three men stared at the images.

"Damn it, Simon, the C-spine series is still bad. I can't tell much. Clear to C-5 and then blurred."

"Don, this guy has really broad shoulders and he's got lots of muscle mass. It is damn hard to see beyond C-5. C-6 and C-7 are here but I agree they're had to read."

The three men continued to stare at the film. From what they could tell, everything appeared to be alright, but they weren't sure.

"I think we should we try again." said Simon.

"No, let's let it go. I think he's OK. We can expect some numbness and weakness due to trauma. I think the real problem is trying to save that foot."

CHAPTER ONE

Late that afternoon Margaret talked to Paul Morales. He told her that Joe was improving. He explained they had put the soft collar around his neck as a precaution, but they felt it would be needed only for a few days. He was honest with Margaret about his concern about Joe's foot. He told her the circulation wasn't good, but that it seemed to be improving slightly. All in all, he told her that Joe was recovering.

Margaret was delighted when Dr. Morales said she could stay with Joe for an hour. He advised her to talk quietly and warned her that Joe was still in a lot of pain.

She saw that Joe was awake when she went into his room. She pulled a chair up close to the bed, sat and reached for Joe's hand. "Hi, sweetheart. How do you feel?"

"Better. Glad you're here," he whispered.

She squeezed his hand and he squeezed back. Margaret was surprised at how weak his grasp felt.

"Maggie, who's taking care of the animals?"

"My mom and dad went to the farm yesterday. They called last night and said everything is OK. Mamma said Barton was really glad to see them. He wagged his tail for an hour."

She saw the broad grin fill Joe's face. He did love that dog. Barton had just shown up at the farm a year ago, thin and scraggly, his coat filled with sand burrs. Margaret fed him and that night Joe spent an hour grooming the dog and talking quietly to him.

They reported the dog to the Humane Society and put an ad in the paper, but there were no inquiries. They named the dog after one of Joe's college roommates, Kelly Barton, who had played football at A & M with Joe. Kelly Barton was smart, tough and a little seedy looking. That seemed to fit the dog.

"What do the doctors say?" asked Joe.

"They say you're doing better. Oh Joe, I was so scared when I first saw you," said Margaret, beginning to cry.

"Hey girl, I'm doing fine. Don't cry."

"I'm sorry. I know you're getting better. Can I do anything for you?"

"No. I just wish I could get more comfortable," answered Joe, almost in a whisper. The oxygen tubes going down his nose sometimes made it difficult for him to talk.

Joe closed his eyes and Margaret was content to sit and hold his hand.

Orelia came in and checked the flow of fluids in the subclavian line. She inserted a needle into the line and injected 4 mg. of morphine to keep ahead of the pain. She took his blood pressure and found it was 130/70. His color was pale and his skin felt warm. His temperature was slightly elevated.

"Mrs. Baxter, the hour is up. I've got to do a few things for Joe right now. You can come back tonight, OK? " said Orelia, smiling.

Margaret nodded and stood. She leaned over and kissed Joe. His eyes fluttered and he smiled at Margaret.

When Margaret left the room, Orelia gave Joe a Tylenol suppository. She checked the catheter and saw it was draining clear, yellow fluid. Her patient seemed a bit better.

Marge Kern looked up from her keyboard as Consuela walked through the door.

"Good Morning," said Marge, smiling.

"Hi. Sorry I'm late. Fred and I stayed up the valley with Mom and Dad until after midnight."

"How's your dad?"

"He's fine. He decided he had to play dominoes," said Consuela, laughing. Marge laughed too. She had worked for the law firm for twenty years, worked with Bill Travis before Consuela had joined the firm. She knew him well.

"Maria insisted that she didn't know where the domino set was but he wouldn't be deterred. All of us had to look, including Fred, while Dad sat in his chair telling us different places to look. Mother finally found the damn things and we started to play. Marge, I want you to know that Maria Fernandez Travis is an ace. She whipped us good! The woman has a mind like a calculator."

Marge laughed and said, "How'd your dad take it?"

"He yelled a lot! But he had a fine time. He may come in later in the week. They're going to the ranch this weekend. He doesn't have anything pressing, does he?"

"No. I went over his calendar with him before he went to the hospital. He's clear for a couple of weeks."

Marge got up and poured coffee for herself and for Consuela. They took the coffee and went into Consuela's office. There was a set of very large tinted windows in the back of Consuela's desk. Mt. Franklin could be seen looming in the background. A light mist hung over the top of the mountain, accenting the deep purple of the rock crevices. Below the mountain, the high desert country gleamed. Freshly washed by the rain, the green of the Mesilla Valley and the Rio Grande bordered by farms and the immense pecan orchards were lush.

"We need to write Mark Harper a letter," said Consuela as she settled herself at her desk.

"What's the story? You saw Mrs Gonzales yesterday, didn't you?"

"Yes. She just can't wait for the money. So, we need to tell Harper that she will accept Jack Porter's offer. It really bothers me because I know I could have gotten a lot more and they really need it. But I'm sure Harper and Porter figured she couldn't wait a couple of years for the money. They were right."

"OK. What time are you going up to the race track with Cynthia?"

"I told her I'd meet her there about ten this morning. Call her and check the time. We have the sales contract all written, right?"

"Yes, I'll bring it in and you can check it over. Why does that lady buy so many horses?" asked Marge, laughing.

Consuela laughed and said, "Cynthia just loves race horses, I guess." Cynthia Hall Steelman had been a classmate of Consuela's at the Radford School. She was tall, rather raw-boned and her hair always looked sun-bleached. She had been unable to persuade her parents to let her go to the University of Texas: her mother insisted she go back east to school and she had gone to Smith. To her great surprise she had loved it. When she was a junior she had met a Dartmouth man who was also from Texas. They had fallen in love and she and Jim Steelman were married the year she graduated.

Jim's father had made a fortune in the oil and natural gas drilling business but had seen the decline coming in drilling in the states and gotten out early. Jim and his father now concentrated on natural gas pipe line construction and liquid natural gas transportation.

Jim spent much of his time out of town and was content to let Cynthia do exactly as she pleased and she pleased to own a string of race horses.

"When you call her, see if Jim's in town. I need to talk to him about that pipeline contract outside of Ft. Stockton," said Consuela.

"Will do. Anything else?" answered Marge.

"That's all I have. You got anything?"

"Just a reminder that you've got to file papers on Thursday in Judge Ward's court on the Martin case."

"Right. I can finish that this morning. I'll give you the disc when I finish and you can proof it and print it. OK?"

"Yep."

"Great. Thanks, Marge."

Marge went back to the outer office and Consuela turned on her computer and started to work.

Joe was awake when Orelia came into the room. He tried to smile but the pain in his arms was really bothering him. His leg hurt too but the pain in his arms really bothered him.

"How are you feeling, Joe?" asked Orelia as she walked to the foot of his bed and glanced at his chart. She saw his vital signs had remained stable all night and he had continued to receive the morphine sulfate.

"My arms hurt," he whispered.

Orelia checked the G-tube. It looked OK. Surely, surely they will remove the G-tube today, she thought. She was sure he could eat now. His breathing had stabilized and they had removed the endotrachael tube a couple of days before. She could see no point in continuing to feed him via the G-tube.

"My arms hurt," repeated Joe.

"Here, try to squeeze my hand, " Orelia said as she walked to the side of the bed and took his hand in hers. The grasp was still weak. She went to the other side and took that hand in hers. "Try to squeeze now."

That grasp was also weak. "I'll get you some more meds, Joe. I think it will help the pain. OK?"

"OK."

Orelia went back to the nurse's station and checked the doctor's notes. The notes mentioned the weak bilateral hand grasp but the doctor's notes didn't indicate any particular concern about that fact. Most of Randy Patterson's notes concerned the electrolyte balance and the blood gas studies. Paul Morales' notes, which were very hard to read, always seemed to focus on the leg and foot. Don Robert's had written some notes too but they too focused on the leg and foot.

Orelia shuffled through all the doctor's notes and was surprised there were no notes from Sam Boswell. He was listed on the chart as the Admitting Doctor and was thus the doctor in charge of Joe's care. She knew he had been out of town during the previous weekend but she had seen him in the hospital this week. Apparently he hadn't checked on Joe.

Orelia gave Joe more morphine sulfate and some Valium. In a few minutes he dozed off. Orelia was sitting in the chair in Joe's room writing notes on his chart when she heard someone at the door. It was Margaret.

"Can I come in?" asked Margaret.

"Sure,"

Joe woke up and turned to look at Margaret.

As he turned his head, they all heard the sound. It was a snap, a pop. Joe's eyes suddenly opened wide. Orelia jumped up and Margaret stood frozen in the doorway.

"What was that?" Margaret asked.

"Joe, are you OK?" Orelia asked, a chill of apprehension running down her spine.

Joe could not speak for a minute. He continued to stare with wide eyes, fear beginning to fill his face.

"I can't move. I can't move!" he whispered.

"Take it easy, Joe. Stay still. I'll call the doctor. Let me just check you for a second," Orelia said as she quickly checked his breathing and other vital signs.

While Orelia checked Joe, Margaret rushed to his side. She was confused and terrified. Orelia grabbed her hand and looked at her.

"Mrs. Baxter. Calm down. You sit here with Joe. Keep him calm while I go get the doctor."

"What's the matter? What happened?"

"I'm not sure. I've got to get the doctor. Now, calm down, OK?"

Margaret nodded and Orelia ran out of the room. When she got to the nurse's station she yelled, "Is Doctor Patterson still on the floor? Or Dr. Morales of Dr. Roberts? Any of Joe Baxter's doctors?"

"No," answered one of the nurses. "Orelia what's the matter?"

"I don't know, but it's not good. I think he's paralyzed," answered Orelia as she reached for the phone. She asked the operator to page Patterson, Morales and Roberts stat. Within a minute the phone rang. Orelia was relieved when she discovered it was Dr. Roberts who had answered the page.

"Dr. Roberts, please come up here, stat. It's Joe Baxter. I think he's paralyzed. He turned his head and there was a loud pop and now he can't move."

Roberts and Paul Morales arrived quickly and rushed to Joe's room. When they entered they saw Orelia and Margaret standing by the bed. Joe looked confused and scared.

"What seems to be the problem, Joe?" asked Roberts as he approached the bed.

"I can't move my right leg and I can't feel my left leg. What's wrong with me?"

Roberts and Paul indicated that Orelia should take Margaret outside. Roberts took a small pin from his jacket. He asked Joe to close his eyes. "I'm going to touch you with something. You tell me when you can feel it, OK?"

Roberts began at the sole of Joe's right foot. He stuck the pin in several places. There was no response. He tried the left big toe which was sticking out of the cast. Still no response. Roberts looked at Paul Morales and frowned. He continued to prick Joe up the groin and belly. Not until he got above Joe's nipples was there any response.

"Joe, let's take you down and get an X-ray so we know what we're dealing with, OK?" said Roberts. He turned to Paul and said, "Go call Orthopedic X-ray and see if we can bring him down right now."

"Doctor, what's the matter?" asked Joe. "Why can't I move? Why can't I feel anything?"

"Joe, I don't know right now. It may be temporary. You sustained a lot of injuries. There may be some swelling that is affecting your spinal column. We'll know when we see the X-rays."

Joe was taken down to X-ray immediately. Later, Simon Webster met Roberts and Morales in the X-ray reading room. They clipped the X-rays up on the lighted box and for the first time they could see clearly down to the seventh cervical vertebra. They were not happy with what they saw. Dr. Webster pointed to C-7 and said, "There it is. That's a displaced fracture if I ever saw one."

"Shit," muttered Roberts.

"He must have popped it when he turned his head this morning," muttered Paul.

"How did he turn his head? Didn't you have him in a hard cervical collar?"

"No we didn't Simon. We had him in a soft collar. If you people had taken a decent X-ray so we could have seen down to C-7 we would have seen the fracture and put him in a hard collar and this wouldn't have happened," answered Roberts.

"What do we do now?" asked Paul.

"Let's put him in a halo traction device and set the traction weight at about forty pounds. Give him a ton of steroids. Maybe if we can hold him still and reduce the swelling the thing will heal and he'll regain feeling. Shit, I hope so."

Joe was given 20 mg. of Dexadron in his IV tube and more morphine sulfate and Valium to keep him calm. Under local anesthesia the halo tongs of the traction brace were screwed into his skull and the base of the brace came down below his chest, almost entirely covering the gastric tube protruding from his stomach.

When he was taken back to his room, Margaret was horrified at the sight of the halo brace. A forty pound weight was attached to the traction device. She tried to talk to Joe but he was confused and drowsy.

Joe's parents were plainly worried and waited with Margaret to talk to the doctors. Dr. Roberts arrived in a few minutes and motioned them to follow him. They went into a conference room.

When they sat down he said, "I've got some bad news for you. Joe turned his head too sharply this morning and there is a displaced fracture of the seventh vertebra. We won't know how serious this is going to be for a few days. We hope the traction and the steroids will reduce the swelling and that feeling will return."

"When will you know if he's going to be able to move again?" asked Joe's father.

"In a few days. We'll do everything we can, Mr. Baxter. You folks just pray."

Chapter Two
The Search

Consuela showed her pass at the entrance to Sunland Park Race Track and drove her car to Cynthia's barn. She saw Cynthia's silver Mercedes and parked next to it.

As she got out of the car she saw an absolutely beautiful bay stallion standing between the barns. His coat was a deep brown and the mane and tail were jet black. A groom was brushing him vigorously and it was obvious the stallion enjoyed the attention.

"Hey, Consuela, isn't he something!" shouted Cynthia as she walked up to the car. Consuela laughed and gave Cynthia a big hug.

"I've got to admit it, Cynthia, this animal is beautiful. At least he looks terrific, but can he run?"

"Girl, this stud is going to be a champion!" Cynthia grabbed Consuela by the hand and drug her over to the horse. "Jose," Cynthia said to the groom, "tell her. Is he good or what?"

"Si, muy bien! This boy he run real good. I think maybe he win everything. Maybe so Miz Steelman have a real winner this time. He sure better than the last one," said Jose and laughed as Cynthia punched his arm.

"Did you bring the contract? I told Tolliver that I wanted the horse today before he snuck some mare with him!"

"I've got it right here in the briefcase. Let's go get it signed before you collapse with excitement."

"I told Tolliver we'd meet him at the kitchen at 10. I think Jim's going to be able to come by this morning too. Shoot, girl, if you're real good I'll even buy you one of those cinnamon buns!"

When they walked into the small café by the gate, there were shouts from several trainers and grooms. The word was clearly out that Cynthia Steelman was going to buy the stallion.

"Hey, Miz Steelman, you gonna run that horse or just pet him?"

Cynthia looked at Bob Spencer, a trainer, and said, "Bob-O, I'll let you pet him after I beat you in the derby!" There were loud shouts and whistles. Cynthia laughed.

They got their coffee and the homemade cinnamon buns and took their trays to the corner table where George Tolliver was sitting. George stood as they approached the table.

"Morning ladies."

"Hi, George," said Cynthia.

The contract was quickly signed and Cynthia left to go to the track office to get the papers filed.

"How long have you known Mrs. Steelman?" George asked.

"Since we were children. Always." Consuela said.

"How did that lady learn so much about horses? Everybody loves to tease her because she's such a good sport, but the truth is she does real good."

"When Cynthia likes something, she does it like a whirlwind. She talks to everybody, reads everything."

"She sure does! I thought she was off her rocker last year when she bought that brown horse, Kikker Boot. I didn't see much in that horse. Didn't see much until he passed my horse at the quarter pole in that stakes race last fall."

"God, old Kikker Boot! Even Jim thought she was nuts on that one. Kikker Boot is now living happily on my dad's ranch, as a matter of fact."

"How is Bill?"

"You know my dad?"

"Miss Travis, everybody knows your dad!" said George, laughing. "As a matter of fact, he represented me in a case about fifteen years ago."

"Did you win?"

"Never even went to trial. Your dad put the fear into those folks and he got me a nice settlement. I admire that man."

"So do I.. I'll tell him hello for you."

Consuela saw Jim Steelman coming through the door and waved. She had always liked Jim and enjoyed working with him. Cynthia was so bright and funny but she had always been headstrong and a meek man could never survive being married to her. Jim was strong and self-confident, self-confident enough not to be threatened by Cynthia. In fact, he relished Cynthia's strength.

When people first met Jim Steelman, they immediately thought that his name fit. Consuela knew that was only partly right. Strong as steel, yes. But warm and cuddly and kind. Perfect for Cynthia.

"Hi, Consuela," Jim said as he came to the table.

"Jim, how are you? Do you know George Tolliver?"

Chapter Two

"Hi. I don't think we've met but Cynthia talks about you a good bit. How are you?"

The two men shook hands warmly. George said goodby and Jim sat with Consuela.

"Where's Cynthia?"

"She's gone to file the sale papers on the horse at the track office. She should be back any minute. Have you seen the horse? He's really beautiful."

"Have I seen the horse? God, yes! Cyn drug me out here Monday when I got in from Houston. Good looking horse, I must admit. Cynthia is really high on this horse and I've learned not to argue with her about horses. She's got some kind of sixth sense. Oh, here she comes."

Cynthia walked up to the table carrying a tray. She leaned over and kissed Jim and gave him some coffee and a cinnamon bun.

"Thought you'd like this," Cynthia said. She had also gotten some fresh coffee for Consuela. "Remember how the Yankees always put so much sugar and cream in their coffee? Always tickled me."

They laughed, as all Texans do, at the strange ways of the Yankees.

Consuela turned to Jim and said, "I've brought the papers on the pipeline outside Ft. Stockton." She handed him a packet.

"Thanks, Consuela. I'll get these back to you tomorrow."

"Consuela," said Cynthia, "have you heard anything else about Joe Baxter?"

"Not since Dad left the hospital. I should call. Margaret seemed encouraged when I saw her."

"You'd like Joe," said Cynthia turning to Jim. "He's a good guy. Went to A & M , but we'll forgive him that lapse. He really is nice. I remember how Margaret got all dreamy-looking whenever she thought about Joe. I always thought the most interesting thing about Margaret was Joe."

"Cyn, that was a tacky thing to say," said Consuela. "Margaret's nice."

"Nice doesn't mean interesting. Of course she's nice. But she was always so meek. God, she was so shy when she first came to Radford. I think she was terrified of D.T."

"We were _all_ terrified of D.T.!" said Consuela, laughing. D.T. was the legendary Dr. Lucinda de Lefwich Templin, the headmistress of Radford for forty years. She was austere, determined, and strict. She had dominated the school until her death. Her memory was still a powerful force.

"Well, that's true. But Margaret couldn't even speak to her."

"Cynthia Hall couldn't either, as I recall. Not when she first came to Radford"

"Clearly there are some disadvantages to lifelong friendships. I can't get away with anything with you. OK, OK, Margaret's terrific!"

"Old toughie here just sent flowers to them this week," said Jim.

"Not surprising. All bark, no bite," said Consuela who grinned at Cynthia.

"I never said I didn't like Margaret. And besides, I sent them to Joe. Good lookin' dude! And speaking of good looking, how's Fred? I'll let him take care of my heart anytime," said Cynthia laughing raucously.

"Cynthia, you're impossible," said Consuela, joining in the laughter. "He's fine. We're going to the ranch this weekend. Want to come?"

"I may have a horse running. I'll check. What about your schedule, Honey"

Jim looked at his appointment book. "Maybe. Maybe. If I can tie up some loose ends by then, I could. I'd love to see Bill and Maria. We'll call you."

Joe was disoriented most of the afternoon. He was given 20 mg of Decadron in hopes the steroid would reduce the swelling, in hopes feeling would return to his body. At 3:30 Orelia Ortiz took his temperature and saw that it was elevated despite the Tylenol she had given to him.

Dr. Morales ordered that blood cultures be drawn at five minute intervals. At least his urine output had remained good. Orelia listened to Joe's lungs with her stethoscope and realized the lungs were becoming congested.

When Margaret saw Joe later in the afternoon she was frightened. The tongs attached to his head formed a bizarre halo and he seemed dwarfed by all the equipment: the leg traction, the hideous tongs attached to his head and the halo device that was attached to something that came down over his chest, the oxygen tubes, the various monitors, other tubes attached somewhere and draining. Joe himself seemed lost in modern medical technology.

Margaret sat down in the chair next to his bed, thinking Joe was asleep. She was surprised when he said her name and she reached for his hand.

"Joe, how do you feel?"

"Terrible."

Chapter Two

Joe started trying to turn his head back and forth despite the tongs. He managed slight turns. Margaret put her hand on his face and said, "Joe, don't do that. I'm here. What can I do to help you?" Joe didn't reply.

Orelia came in the room and put her arms around Margaret's shoulders, giving her a firm squeeze and said, "Pretty scary looking equipment, I know. But, Mrs Baxter, we're doing everything we can. In some ways he is better. The pain is gone from his arms and he can move them."

"What about his legs?"

"Nothing yet. I'm sorry. We hope when the swelling is reduced, sensation will return."

Suddenly, Joe began trying to turn his again. It moved only slightly but he kept trying. Orelia touched him and told him to relax. Joe kept turning his head.

"I'm going to have to get some small sandbags to put on either side of his head to keep him still. I'll be right back."

Margaret stood and looked down at Joe, tears filling her eyes.

The next morning Orelia stood at the nurse's station reading the night reports on Joe Baxter. He had remained agitated most of the night despite a stiff injection of Valium. His lungs were more congested and apparently the left upper lobe had collapsed. Only gross body movements were observed. His temperature was elevated.

"God," thought Orelia, "This guy is having a terrible time."

As she walked down the hall toward Joe's room, she saw Dr. Patterson and hurried to catch up.

Randy stopped and smiled at her. He had just come from early surgery and wanted to check on some patients before returning to the operating room.

"What can I do for you? I've only got a few minutes. I've got to check on Mrs. Talbott and then get back to the OR."

"Have you talked to Dr. Boswell about Joe Baxter?"

"Just briefly this morning. He was sorry to hear about the paralysis."

"What about the agitation and the elevated temperature?"

"Let's see what the blood cultures show. Talk to Dr. Roberts."

Orelia shook her head and walked to Joe's room. She hated it when a patient was being cared for by two sets of doctors. The surgeons kept telling her to talk to the orthopods and the orthopods kept telling her to talk to the surgeons. The nurses had to take care of the whole patient but nobody listened to the nurses.

Consuela awakened early Saturday morning as she always did when she was at the ranch. She and Fred had driven from El Paso to the ranch late Friday afternoon, a drive filled with intense sunshine that slowly faded by the time they approached the Davis Mountains, so that the mountains seemed in dark purples and blues.

Consuela stretched in bed and looked out the window at the willow tree outside. The new leaves were almost chartreuse in the early morning light. She could hear a red-wing blackbird in the distance and a mockingbird nearby who seemed to be warbling an aria from some opera.

She got out of bed and put on an old pair of Levis and a soft cotton shirt. She found her old boots and some socks and put them on. She walked softly to the kitchen so as not to awaken anyone.

Consuela made coffee and took a cup and thermos of coffee outside. She walked across the front yard to some chairs that sat on a bluff overlooking a small lake. She poured some coffee and sat, watching the bass in the lake slowly rising to the surface to feed on the early morning insects.

No wonder, she thought, that my parents love it here so much. Somehow, on the ranch and away from all the noise and sounds of the city, you could stop long enough to notice the world, take time to watch the sunlight and clouds play tag across the surface of the earth, notice new growth in the trees in the early morning sun, hear the birds calling. Thank you God, she thought, for all your creation.

Consuela closed her eyes and felt the sun on her face, felt a slight breeze scurry by from the lake. She heard a horse in the barn banging on the stall gate. She smiled, wondering if it was Molly. Molly had always been what Marie called "an eager eater", what Bill called "a piggy eater". Probably was Molly wanting some grain. She may eat a lot, thought Consuela, but by damn she had the softest back of any horse in the barn, the only horse that Consuela ever rode bareback.

Consuela opened her eyes when she heard a fish jump in the lake. She looked at the surface and saw the slowly spreading circles where the fish had jumped.

"Boo," someone said in back of her. She turned and saw her father standing with a cup in his hand. "Hey, girl, share some with your old Dad."

Consuela laughed and poured him a full cup. He settled down in the chair next to her. "Thought I'd find you out here," he said.

They both drank coffee and looked with pride at the land they loved. Within the next hour they were joined by Maria and Fred. They ate breakfast outside and then Consuela decided to join her father as he rode to a large pasture that bordered the mountains on the southern part of the ranch.

They saddled their horses and started for the pasture. "By the way," said Bill, "Kikker Boot is in that pasture. Wait 'till you see how fat he's gotten."

"Good. I want to see him. Cynthia asked me about him the other day. You think she should breed him?"

"Well, he's good looking. But I always believe that looks come from the sire but the heart to run comes from the dam. Wish he were a mare. I'd sure as hell breed him then. If Cynthia and Jim get here this afternoon we'll talk about it."

"Daddy, does the doctor know you intended to ride horseback this weekend?"

"Hell no! You don't think I was foolish enough to ask permission, do you?"

"Well, be careful. No galloping."

"Who'd want to gallop on a beautiful day like this? I just want to look at things, to see how many wild flowers are in bloom."

They rode across the high desert plains and slowly up the rolling foothills toward the high mountains. They stopped now and then to check the fence line or to look at some cattle. When they reached the pasture that held Kikker Boot, they dismounted and drank coffee from the thermos. They decided to lead Kikker Boot back to the house in case Cynthia came.

They got back to the ranch house a little past noon and went to find Fred and Maria. They were in the patio playing cards. Consuela noticed immediately that they both had wet hair and she started to laugh.

"You didn't! Did you go swimming in the lake?" she asked.

Both Fred and Maria laughed and nodded their heads. "Damn near froze to death," chortled Fred.

"Que suave! I feel like a million bucks," laughed Maria. "Fred decided to go in and I wasn't about to let him go in alone and then have to listen to him all weekend about what a chicken I am. So I went too!"

Cynthia and Jim arrived just before sunset. Cynthia was exuberant as one of her horses had won a stakes race. They arrived with a magnum of champagne and dinner was loud and festive.

After dinner, as they sat outside in the chairs overlooking the lake, Cynthia asked Fred if he knew anything about Joe Baxter.

"No, I'm sorry. I've been swamped all week with surgery. One of my partners has been out of town and I've had to cover for him. I'll try to remember to check on Joe this week."

Consuela spent the first part of the next week preparing for a trial. The case, a messy child custody suit, had been pending for more than a year. Consuela represented the father and they had been ready to go to trial for months but the opposing lawyer had filed endless requests for postponement. Consuela didn't particularly like her client or the mother of the child and she had spent a great deal of time trying to keep them from using the child as a battering ram for their emotions. In her opinion, the case wasn't so much about the custody of the child as it was an arena for two grown people to act like children. Unfortunately, she felt the opposing lawyer was also acting petulant. Come to think of it, Consuela could feel some petulance too.

She wanted to get the case over with. Her father had warned her about "domestic" cases. They were always loaded with hidden emotional layers that un-peeled like an onion at unexpected times. She had taken this case as a favor to a friend and she vowed not to do another "domestic".

The trial lasted three days. It was just as awful as Consuela imagined it would be. She took no pleasure in the fact that she had won the case. She wasn't at all sure her client would be a good father, but she was convinced he would be better for the child than the mother. Marginally. Poor kid.

After the trial, Consuela flew to Austin for a meeting of the State Bar Association. Fred had been asked to consult on a case in San Antonio and they decided to meet in Austin for the weekend.

They rented a car on Sunday to drive out to the hill country. The land was covered in patches of blue bonnets, Indian paint brushes and a variety of other wild flowers in yellows and purples. They stopped the car at a rest area and sat under a live-oak tree and looked out over the hills at Lake Travis. They could see dozens of sail boats, some with spinnaker sails unfolded.

Chapter Two

"There are times when I wished I lived in Austin," said Consuela. "This is one of those times."

"God, me too. This is gorgeous."

"Only thing is," said Consuela, "Not much decent Mexican food here. Some good tamales way out on First street. Decent chorizo at Cisco's. That's about it."

Fred laughed and agreed. He had now lived in El Paso long enough to understand Mexican food and to know the difference between Mexican food and Tex-Mex. There was nothing to compare with the mole sauce at Julio's in Juarez that you dreamed about, or the chile con carne at Grigg's or the baked enchiladas at Leo's.

They got hungry thinking about Mexican food and decided to eat. So, Austin had poor Mexican food, they agreed. They considered the other alternatives. The Sunday buffet at Green Pastures was heavenly but they had missed that. Besides they weren't dressed properly. Maybe some cajun? What about barbecue? Austin did have decent barbecue. How about hamburgers at Dirty Martin's, their college hangout? Or burgers and hand cut French fries at the Waterloo Ice House? They considered the range of new up-scale yuppie places but finally decided to head out to the Paleface Store and have barbecue.

They ate their barbecue and drank long neck Lone Star beer at a table under the trees. They laughed as they remembered some wild parties while they were undergraduates.

Later that night, Fred talked to Consuela again about getting married. They had this conversation periodically. Neither could imagine that they wouldn't get married someday. But when? Soon, they decided. Soon.

Sometime during the next month Consuela thought about Joe Baxter and realized she had not talked to Margaret in weeks. Surely Joe must be back home by now and well on his way to recovery. When she had last seen Margaret, while her father was still in the hospital, she had seemed hopeful.

Consuela put down the deposition she was reading and reached over and picked up the phone. She dialed information and asked about a listing for Joe Baxter. She told the operator that he lived on a farm somewhere down the valley.

"Hmm. Nothing in El Paso or Ysleta. Just a second. Could this be it? Joe and Margaret Baxter in San Elizario?"

"Bingo!"

Consuela dialed the number and let the phone ring a dozen times. Perhaps they were outside, she thought. Consuela hung up. She made a note of the telephone number and promised herself she would try later.

Consuela and Fred invited Bill and Maria and Cynthia and Jim to have dinner with them at Consuela's house in Kern Place. Cynthia told Jim for days before the dinner she was sure Fred and Consuela were going to announce their wedding plans at the dinner. Jim was not convinced, telling Cynthia, "Cyn, you just love them so much you want them to get married. I want them to also...but I'll bet it is just a dinner party. Consuela just wants to try out some new gourmet item she has discovered."

The dinner was grand, a feast of Steak Diane which Consuela prepared in a chaffing dish at the table, with the appropriate flourishes as she added lemon juice or sherry to loud applause.

During dessert, a light chocolate mousse, Fred uncorked a large bottle of Cristal champagne. Cynthia screamed when she saw the bottle, "I knew it. By God, I knew it! If this were just a nice dinner we'd be having some regular champagne. Cristal! Come on. Tell us!"

Fred and Consuela started laughing. Maria looked puzzled for a minute and then she grabbed Bill's hand and beamed.

"We have something to tell you," started Consuela but she was drowned out by loud hoops and shouts from Cynthia.

Fred had to shout, "We're getting married!"

Everyone started to hug everyone else. Maria and Cynthia and Consuela were all crying. So was Bill. Fred and Jim kept shaking hands.

Finally, Bill grabbed the bottle of champagne, poured some for everyone and yelled, "I propose a toast."

All stood with raised glasses as Bill said, "Baby girl, you make me real proud. Your mamma and I love you and you know we love Fred like a son. Who else would swim in the lake with Maria?" There was laughter and cheering.

"Fred," continued Bill, " I welcome you to the family. I pray that you will be as happy as Maria and I. You take care of Consuela. And Consuela, you take care of Fred. We love you both. Thank God, you've finally decided to make an honest woman of my daughter."

Cynthia shouted and laughed and they all drank the champagne. Cynthia and Jim immediately agreed to serve as Matron of Honor and Best Man. Maria said Consuela could wear the beautiful handmade bridal gown that she had worn when she married Bill. Bill announced he was going to throw "one hell of an engagement party."

Consuela tried to reach Margaret and Joe Baxter to invite them to the engagement party. No one answered the phone. Finally, Consuela sent them an invitation in the mail but on the night of the party they did not attend nor did they respond to the invitation.

The party was a smash. Bill Travis pulled out all the stops for the engagement party for his only child. Maria, wearing a stunning traditional mantilla around her shoulders, made her way easily among all the guests. After midnight, Cynthia talked to the orchestra, they struck up a conga tune and she lead the huge crowd in a conga line, the first conga line in El Paso in at least a decade. By the time the crowd was finished they was both exuberant and exhausted. Those who stuck it out were served an elegant champagne breakfast and the band, also needing a change of pace, played quiet old standards while the guests ate.

Finally, the party wound down. The staff of the Country Club was exhausted, but they all loved the Travis family. Many of them had known the family for years and Bill and Consuela had helped many of them with legal problems. Maria was always considerate and the Hispanic members of the staff admired the way she moved with equal ease among all groups of people.

When Fred took Consuela home after the party, they sat in the early morning light in the patio drinking coffee. They talked about the wedding, about how their life would be together, how many children they should have. They made plans to go look at a house in the upper valley later in the week. They wanted to buy a house and get it furnished before the wedding.

They had talked a lot lately about how to manage their two busy careers and their marriage. They knew there might be stresses when Fred was especially busy with surgery and when Consuela had difficult litigation pending. Fortunately, not only were they in love, but they were truly best friends and that friendship would best serve to help them through difficult times.

The next Friday afternoon, Consuela decided to drive to the ranch. She needed Bill to sign some papers and she wanted to go over wedding plans with Maria. Fred couldn't go with her, so early in the afternoon Consuela started for the ranch.

She saw an exit sign on the Interstate for San Elizario. On an impulse, she decided to try to find Joe and Margaret. She stopped at a service station on the edge of town. "I wonder if you can help me," she asked. "I'm looking for Joe and Margaret Baxter's farm. Do you know where it is?"

The attendant gave her a peculiar look, nodded and said, "Yeah, just down this road about two miles. You'll see a sign that says 'Baxter Farms'."

Consuela thanked him and started down the road. She hadn't been in San Elizario since she was a child. Sometimes, when she and her parents were going back to El Paso from the ranch, they had exited the Interstate and had driven up the "old road" and she remembered Bill and Maria telling her how beautiful it used to be with the huge old cottonwood trees forming an arch over the road for miles and miles, what a relief from the heat that shade gave them before cars had air conditioning. Maria had told her that Juan de Onate had been in San Elizario in the 1500's and that it was part of Mexico until the Rio Grande river shifted. Consuela saw that San Elizario didn't have many of the old cottonwood trees but it did have stores and bakeries and businesses that sold farm supplies and equipment. She passed by the Chihuahua Bakery and thought she might stop there on the way out of town and see if they had some pan dulces she could take to her mother.

She saw the farm sign and turned on to the dirt road leading to the house and barn. There was a car parked by the house. She hoped they were home.

When she parked the car, a large, friendly dog barked and ran up to greet her, wagging his tail. Consulea got out of the car and reached down to give the dog a pat. She heard the door open and looked up and saw Margaret standing in the doorway.

"Hi Margaret," she said.

Margaret looked awful. She had lost weight. Her eyes were sunken. She looked at Consuela for a minute and then burst into tears.

"Margaret, what's the matter?" Consuela asked as she rushed to her friend. "Is Joe alright?"

Margaret continued to cry as Consuela put her arms around her friend. "Margaret, what's wrong?"

"Joe's dead."

Consuela stepped back in shock. She stared at Margaret. She couldn't comprehend what Margaret had said. Surely not. That couldn't be, she thought. "Margaret, what are you saying?"

"He's dead. Gone"

"My God. When? What happened?"

"He died six weeks ago. In the hospital."

"But I thought he was getting better. The last time I saw you in the hospital you said he was getting better. What happened?"

Margaret started sobbing and could barely say, "I don't know. He got paralyzed and then he got infected. He just died."

Consuela took Margaret's hand and lead her into the house. They sat on the couch in the living room. Consuela tried to comfort her. After awhile, Margaret regained her composure but the look of pain never left her face.

"Margaret, try to tell me what happened."

"Connie, I really don't know. I kept asking the doctors but I couldn't understand what they were saying. The first thing that went wrong was that Joe turned his head and fractured a vertebrae. That left him paralyzed from the chest down. They put him in a huge brace thing that screwed into his scalp and went down below his chest. But it didn't help."

"But why did he die? You don't die from paralysis."

"He got some kind of infection and he just got worse and worse. They did some operations, but nothing helped."

Margaret started crying again. "I just wish I could understand why he died," she said though sobs. "I just wish I could understand. It was so awful."

"Margaret, do you want me to try to find out? I can have Fred look at his records and then maybe I can explain it to you. Would that help?"

"Oh, yes!" said Margaret, relief flooding her face. "If I could just understand it, it would help."

Consuela stayed with Margaret for several hours, trying to offer help and support. She asked if Margaret was financially secure, if she needed anything. Margaret told her that Joe had a small insurance policy but that the company still hadn't paid her. She asked if Consuela could write the company to see what the delay was. Consuela quickly said she would and offered to loan Margaret some money in the meantime. Margaret declined. Consuela had the feeling she declined out of pride.

"Are you going to be able to keep the farm?"

"I don't know. I try to think about it but I just can't."

"Do you have an accountant?"

"Yes. I'm supposed to see him this week. I guess he'll be able to tell me something. Joe trusted him and my dad is going to go with me."

"Good. Margaret, let me copy the information about the insurance. I'm on my way to the ranch and I have to go. Will you go with me? My parents would love to see you."

"Thank you, but I can't. I have chores to do."

"OK. I'll write the insurance company Monday morning. In fact, I'll call them and write them. I'll get Fred to look at Joe's records Monday. I'll give you a call when I find out anything. Margaret, I'm so sorry Joe is gone. I still can't believe it."

On Monday, Consuela called the insurance agent. He said he would look up the Baxter file and call her back. She said she'd hold on line while he looked at the file. In a few minutes he said it would still be several weeks before the claim was paid.

"But Joe Baxter died six weeks ago."

"I'm aware of that, Miss Travis."

"When did you get confirmation of his death?"

"Shortly after he died."

"Then what's the delay?"

"It just takes time to process these claims."

"Mr. Kelly, I am writing you a letter today and I will be sending a copy to the state insurance commissioner. This kind of delay is unconscionable. Margaret Baxter needs the money. She is entitled to a prompt payment. Is there something you're not telling me, some problem?"

"No, not really."

"Mr. Kelly, I urge you to get on this thing right now. Margaret is entitled to be paid the death benefits."

"I'll see what I can do."

"Please do. I don't want to get into a brouhaha with you over this, but I will if she is not promptly paid."

Consuela hung up the phone. She was steaming. Insurance companies drove her to distraction when they failed to pay legitimate claims promptly. They'd sure cut you off if you failed to pay the premium on time, but thought nothing about dragging their heels when it was time to pay out.

CHAPTER TWO

That night Fred told her he had looked at Joe Baxter's medical records. "Not all the records were there, but what happened was that Joe fractured his sixth vertebrae which left him paralyzed. After that he developed a systemic infection and it simply couldn't be controlled. Poor guy suffered a lot. It took a couple of weeks for him to die of the infection."

"But why did he get the infection?"

"I don't know Consuela. There are so many staph germs floating around every hospital. He was in a weakened condition and just couldn't fight off the infection."

"What do you mean that not all the records were there?"

"It wasn't a complete set of records."

"What was missing?"

"Margaret, I really can't discuss his record with you. That's confidential information. You know I looked at the record as a favor to Margaret."

"Fred, for God's sake, what is going on?"

"Consuela, I don't think anything is going on. Because of medical ethics, I can't discuss this any further. I wasn't his doctor and his records are confidential. You wouldn't discuss one of your clients cases with me because of the same rules of confidentiality. Come on, admit it."

Consuela, who had begun to be irritated with Fred, stopped short. Fred was right. She wouldn't discuss certain things with Fred about her clients. Perhaps she shouldn't even have asked him to look at Joe's files.

"Touche. Fred, I'm sorry. You're right. I shouldn't have asked you to even look at his files. I won't ask you to do any such thing again. I just thought you could look at them and then we could explain them to Margaret and give her some comfort. She really is haunted by the fact she doesn't understand what happened."

"I know, honey. That's why I looked. Just tell her what I said, he got a systemic infection that couldn't be controlled. These things happen."

When Consuela called Margaret the next day she told her what Fred had said.

"I know that, Consuela. What I still can't understand is how he could fracture his neck when he was in the hospital. How did he get the infection? Can you ask Fred about that?"

"Margaret, I really can't. Joe wasn't Fred's patient and medical ethics prevent Fred from talking about Joe's case. Do you understand?"

"Yes. I guess I do. But how am I ever going to understand what happened to Joe."

"Margaret, if you want me to, I'll get Joe's records and look at them. As your attorney, I can do that. You'll have to authorize the hospital to release them to me. Do you want to do that?"

"Yes. Yes, I do. Not understanding is driving me crazy. Somehow I feel that if I could understand, I could accept Joe's death. The whole thing is such a nightmare and I feel so helpless because I could tell he was dying and I couldn't understand why. Something just wasn't right about what the doctors were saying. Connie, please get the records and see if you can understand."

"OK, I'll get right on it. I'll transfer this call to Marge Kern, our secretary, and she'll tell you what to do to get the records released to me. And I do have some good news for you. When I came in today there was a message from your insurance guy, Mr. Kelly. He said your claim had been processed. You should get a check by the end of the week."

"Connie, thank you! That will really help. What do I owe you?"

Consuela laughed, "Not a thing. I'm happy to do it for you. What are classmates and friends for? Actually, let me charge you $5 so I can be your official paid attorney on these matters."

Margaret laughed and said, "A deal! I'll send the check this morning."

Consuela wrote the Medical Records Office at the hospital and asked that they send a copy of Joe Baxter's medical records. She got a call a few days later and the head clerk told her the records were extensive and asked if she wanted the whole set. Consuela said she did.

"Does this have anything to do with a case?" the clerk asked.

"No, why do you ask?"

"Well, copying this record is going to cost a lot of money. You sure you want the whole thing?"

Consuela was puzzled. The clerk seemed stiff and formal. But she had promised Margaret so she asked for an estimate of the charges for copying the records. The amount was rather large but she said, "Yes, please copy the complete record. I'll pay the entire charge."

When the records arrived they were extensive. Consuela groaned as she hefted the records on to the large table in her office. But Margaret was her friend and perhaps if she could make some basic sense of the records she could explain to Margaret why Joe had died, she could give her the comfort of knowing.

She picked up the first stack and started reading. It took Consuela three days to get through the records, reading between clients, reading at night, reading steadily until she finished.

Chapter Two

She was shocked by the record. She certainly didn't understand it all but she understood enough to see the suffering that Joe Baxter had endured. No, not endured. Had endured and then had died.

But some things about the record puzzled Consuela. Something wasn't quite right. Before she talked to Margaret she would have to re-read some sections to answer questions that were forming in her mind. She couldn't yet say why Joe had died. From infection, yes. But something wasn't right. She wanted to understand so she could clearly explain it to Margaret.

Consuela began to draw up a list of questions, a list of things she didn't understand. She realized that much of the record was unclear to her because of her lack of medical knowledge. She'd had two medical malpractice cases and had acquired some sense of basic hospital and medical practices. But much in Joe Baxter's case was new to her and she wasn't in a position to know if any malpractice was involved. She certainly hoped not. She just wanted to understand so she could help her friend.

She was troubled by two facts: Joe had arrived at the hospital seriously injured but not paralyzed. Joe had apparently arrived without infection and yet it was infection that had killed him. For Margaret's sake she had to figure out what happened. Maybe then Consuela could figure out what was bothering her about the medical record. She couldn't put her finger on it, but something wasn't right.

She made a note on a legal pad, the first of many questions she would try to answer.

Why was the soft collar placed around Joe's neck at the scene of the accident?

The question triggered a memory. Hadn't the Nurse's Progress Report had multiple entries about numbness before Joe became paralyzed? Flipping through the Nurse's Progress Report she found an entry that said a soft collar had been placed around Joe's neck. She looked at the date. It was several days after Joe had been admitted. Why had the EMT placed a collar on Joe at the scene but the doctors at the hospital had removed it during surgery and had not replaced it for several days?

Did this mean anything? Obviously the EMT at the scene thought there might be a neck injury. Why? The cut on the forehead? Was it standard procedure to place a cervical collar when there was a cut on the forehead in an automobile accident? She decided to call the Medivac people and ask.

She got the shift supervisor on the phone and said, "Hi, this is Consuela Travis. I'm an attorney and I need some general information about your standard procedures."

"Are you going to sue us?"

"No," laughed Consuela. "I'm just curious about what conditions lead you to place a cervical collar on someone injured in a car wreck."

"You mean in general? What does our manual say?"

"Yes. Could you tell me?"

"Just a second. Hold on. I've got a call coming in."

Consuela waited a couple of minutes and the woman came back on the line. "OK," she said, "Here it is. Page 48, under Neck Injuries. 'If the patient complains of neck pain or if there are lacerations on the head, place a soft collar around the patient's neck."

"Do you know why you would do that if there are cuts on the head?"

"Well, because that is often a sign that the head has hit something and therefore the cervical spine may have been injured."

"Would it be possible for me to get a copy of that manual?"

"Sure. Let me give you the name and publisher's address and you can order one."

Consuela took the information, thanked the lady and hung up.

Now, the question was why had the hospital removed the collar and then several days later replaced it? She went back through the Doctor's Progress Reports. It was tough reading. One of the doctors wrote so poorly that she could make out only an occasional word. There were endless orders for lab studies and medications.

There were apparently two different sets of doctors looking after Joe: a surgical team and an orthopedic team. One group concentrated on the internal injuries and breathing and the other concentrated on the leg injuries. No one seemed concerned about the cut on the head.

She looked back at the Operating Room Notes and found that the head injury had been stitched. Apparently that was all the surgeons had thought necessary.

She picked up the Nurse's Progress Reports again. Right from the start the nurses had been concerned with Joe's complaints of numbness and weak bilateral hand grasp. Consuela had found only an occasional mention of this in the doctors notes. What had persuaded them to finally place another soft collar around Joe's neck? Should they have done it earlier? What exactly had Joe done in the hospital that caused the paralysis? What had happened?

She looked at the Admission Notes again. The admission form had been filled out in the Emergency Room. They indicated that Joe had been "involved in a head-on AA" She knew that meant in a head-on automobile accident. The form indicated that the patient had "multiple trauma" and listed under the complaints:

> "Pain and difficulty breathing. Oxy. administered at scene. Rt. Chest pain and mild abdominal pain. Had BP 90 by palpation. Skin laceration RT forehead 3cm/3cm. Soft collar placed at scene. Left leg laceration and multiple fracture at femur. Unable to move leg. Left foot multiple laceration and fracture bone penetration."

The notes also contained orders for fluids and blood studies and for various X-rays. It was noted that a chest tube had been placed.

Consuela re-read the records from the initial surgical procedures. God, Joe had been in really terrible shape. The surgeons had, without doubt, saved his life. He was bleeding internally, had multiple internal injuries and fractures. Consuela was not an expert but even a layman could tell that except for the quick and skilled efforts of the doctors, Joe Baxter would have died and died pretty quickly.

So, what had happened after the surgery? Was it inevitable that Joe was going to die, despite the surgery? Consuela didn't think so. Joe was apparently improving. Margaret had told her that at the hospital coffee shop. He was, at that time, no doubt, still in serious condition. But he was improving. What went wrong? And what the hell caused the paralysis? Why did they put the soft collar back on before the paralysis?

Her secretary, Marge Kern, walked in and gave her some papers to sign. "How's it going?" she asked.

"Tough going. I still can't figure out exactly what happened to Joe," Consuela answered.

"You told me to remind you that the Stewarts will be here at two this afternoon. I'll bring their folder in."

"Thanks."

Consuela wrote a few more notes on her legal pad about Joe's case. She needed to track the soft collar business through the entire record. She needed to read the radiology reports again and see what they said about the cervical spine. Maybe she should call Margaret and tell her it would be a few days before she could tell her exactly why Joe died.

This wasn't going to be as easy as she had assumed. But Consuela was now interested in solving the mystery. Perhaps there wasn't a mystery. Perhaps she just didn't know enough to understand the medical record. That was a challenge. And Consuela Travis loved challenges.

She stood up and moved the three volumes of Joe's medical records to a side table. She stood looking out the window at the mountain, watching the shadow of a cloud glide across the top. She turned after a moment and sat down just as Marge came in with the Stewart folder.

That night Fred came over for dinner. Consuela made primavera with fresh, small asparagus, tomatoes and tiny pieces of broccoli. She tossed the pasta and vegetables with a sauce made from olive oil, fresh basil and finely diced garlic. Fred had brought a dry white wine.

After dinner, it was cool enough to sit in Consuela's patio where they had coffee and Drambuie. Consuela loved to roll the Drambuie around her tongue, tasting the sweet sharpness of the Scotch liquor. The stuff was downright sensual.

Consuela wanted to talk to Fred about Joe's case, but knew that she shouldn't. No point in putting Fred in conflict about medical ethics.

Fred was tired. She knew he had a difficult day in surgery. She snuggled closer and he put his arm around her and gave her a mighty squeeze. They laughed.

"How are you feeling?"

"Much better! Great dinner, the night's cooling down, I'm sitting here with you in my arms. Perfect. How about you?"

"Terrific, " said Consuela as she turned her head to kiss him.

The kiss was long and sweet. They had know each other so long, been in love so long, that they understood that not all kissing led to passion, to making love. It was one of the things that Fred had come to appreciate, the knowledge that love and the expression of love could take so many forms. Often their love-making was eager and wildly passionate, rising to an explosion that left them both staggered. At other times, the love-making was slow and exquisite, both delaying pleasure for as long as possible so that the release, when it came, was more like a rising tide than an explosion. At still other times, like tonight, they took pleasure in being close, in kissing and holding each other, knowing such expressions would lead to deep love but not to love-making.

After awhile, Consuela poured them both more hot coffee and Drambuie. She kissed Fred's nose and put the Drambuie in from of him.

"Well, sport. Do we buy the house or not?" asked Fred.
"I'm still not sure, are you?"
"Not really. I like a lot about it but not everything."
"Fred, I've just had a crazy idea. Let's build!"
"Oh God, Consuela, you're nuts!"
"No. Just listen a minute. You know that lot near the house we looked at? The one down the road. I think there's about an acre of land there."

"The land with the cottonwood and pecan trees? Nice land, I'll admit."

"What if we bought that and designed a house. Made it just what we want. Baked adobe, huge patio, lots of Mexican tile...what do you think?"

Fred smiled, attracted to the idea. "What if we had some stained glass windows, Bougainville vines in the patio..?"

Consuela laughed and nodded her head.

Fred said, "What about the wedding? I doubt we can get it built before we get married."

"No sweat. You move in here until the house is built. Or I'll move in with you."

"That would be OK, wouldn't it. Actually, we might be able to hire a contractor and pay him extra to hire more workers and get the house built quickly."

"Great! Oh Fred. Let's do it. Ah," Consuela suddenly stood up. "I've got a great idea! Let's have all the rooms open to a tiled hallway that circles the patio. A big, wide walkway. Have the roof line hang over the walkway, maybe ten feet wide. We can put furniture here and there around the walkway, make it a livable space too. The patio can have thick St. Augustine grass and we can leave one of those big pecan trees standing inside the patio."

"Love it! Let's also put a pool inside the patio! We can walk right out the door of the bedroom, cross your tiled walkway and do a little skinny dipping. What say?"

"Fantastic! Let's go inside and get some paper. Let's try to draw what we see and see if we can find an architect to do it."

"You got it," said Fred, standing. "I'll find out tomorrow who owns that land and see if we can buy it. Know any architects?"

"You bet!"

The next day Consuela called Margaret Baxter. She didn't want to worry Margaret, didn't want her to know that she thought something was wrong about Joe's medical record. But she suspected that something major was wrong, perhaps even malpractice...but at the moment she couldn't say what was wrong. Certainly she couldn't yet explain to Margaret whether Joe had died from his injuries and the inevitable or probable complications or whether something had gone terribly wrong with his medical care. She was suspicious but that was all and she certainly wasn't ready to share that with Margaret. This wasn't a legal case, just a favor. If she decided there was a legal case there would be plenty of time to discuss that with Margaret.

"Hi, Margaret," Consuela said when she got her on the phone.

"Oh, Connie. How are you? Do you know anything yet?"

"Margaret, not quite yet. I do have the medical records and I have read them. But I haven't yet figured out some parts. What is clear is what you already know. Joe became paralyzed and then got the raging infection which ultimately killed him. But I've still got some questions. I'll get back to you by the end of the week. OK?"

"Sure. And Connie, I really do appreciate you're doing this for me. I can't tell you how much."

"Glad to do it. How are you getting along?"

"Not bad, I guess. I'm not used to Joe being gone. I keep thinking he's about to walk through the door. I guess I haven't accepted his death yet. I hope, if you can tell me why he died, I will accept it."

"I hope so. Listen, Cynthia Steelman is giving a luncheon for me in a couple of weeks. When she asked me who I wanted to invite, I included your name. Is that OK?"

"Connie, I'm flattered. I'm not sure I'm up to going to parties yet."

"Margaret, I know. I do understand, but you should try. You've got to start seeing people again. At least at the luncheon you'll know almost everyone. Think about it, OK?"

"Connie, I will. I promise. Thank you."

When they hung up, Consuela thought about the despair that Margaret must be feeling. God, if anything happened to Fred she didn't know how she would take it. Not well, probably. What was going to happen to Margaret? The insurance money wouldn't last forever. Could she run the farm without Joe? Clearly, Margaret needed to get out, to see people.

Consuela called Cynthia, hoping to catch her at home.

"Hello," she said when Cynthia answered the phone. "Hey, Miz Steelman, how do?"

"God, if it isn't that shyster lawyer," laughed Cynthia. "What's up?"

"Listen, I just talked to Margaret. I told her you were going to invite her to the luncheon. She's uncertain about whether she will come. I think she is just sitting around the house all day, alone. I don't think she goes out at all. Give her a call and see if you can twist her arm."

"I'm sorry to hear that. Poor thing. It really is rotten that Joe died. I still can't believe it. Give me her number and I'll give her a call. Maybe we should drive down there and get her out of the house."

"Really good idea. I'm booked until Friday. What about you?"

"Let's see. I don't have a horse running on Friday. Sure. Let's do it then. Should we tell her we're coming?"

"No. She'll just make up some excuse if we call ahead of time." OK."

"Talk to you later."

When Consuela hung up she worked busily for a couple of hours trying to clear her desk so she could look at Joe's medical record again.

On Thursday, as Consuela was looking over Joe's record again she suddenly realized that the Discharge Note was missing. Could that be? She knew, from her previous cases, that the hospital required the doctor in charge of the patient to write a Discharge Note whether the patient was actually discharged or died.

Perhaps she had missed the note in the almost thousand page set of medical records the hospital had sent. She didn't remember seeing it, but she decided to check through the entire record to make sure.

Consuela quickly looked through the record, briefly glancing at every page. There was no Discharge Note.

Who should have written the note, she wondered. She looked at a page and saw that Boswell, MD was at the top of the page. She leafed through several dozen pages and saw Boswell's name stamped on every page. She went back to the admitting form and saw that Sam Boswell, MD was the admitting doctor. She knew that the admitting doctor normally was the doctor in overall charge of the patient's care even if other doctors were involved. He apparently had remained the doctor in charge throughout Joe's stay.

Consuela didn't remember seeing Boswell's name much in the extensive Doctor's Progress reports. She picked up that section of the record again and started through it, looking for Boswell's name.

Boswell had been involved in the initial surgery. Although his name was on every page as the admitting doctor, she didn't see his name in the body of the record for two weeks. Two weeks! My God, she thought, how is that possible? Be careful, she cautioned herself. Don't jump to conclusions. There was a doctor who wrote so illegibly that she could read only an occasional word. Maybe that was Boswell. Maybe one of the other doctors became the doctor in charge and they just hadn't changed it on the plastic card used at the top of every page.

She searched the record until she found an entry by the doctor who wrote so poorly. She stared at the signature. She really couldn't make out the name. But the first letter was fairly clear and it was an "M". Maybe Marvel? Certainly not Boswell.

What the hell was going on? Virtually every page of the medical record listed Boswell as the admitting doctor and yet he wrote no notes at all during the first two weeks of Joe's hospitalization. After that, he wrote only an occasional note. The doctors who appeared to be in charge were Patterson, Roberts and some doctor whose writing she couldn't read. The few words she could read seemed to refer to orthopedic problems.

She studied the notes. Patterson was apparently a surgeon. She knew Roberts and he was an orthopedic surgeon. She kept reading and saw an entry by Roberts that said Dr. Morales would follow-up on the leg cast problem. She realized the bad handwriting guy was Morales.

She picked up a telephone book and looked in the yellow pages under "Physicians and Surgeons". Boswell was a surgeon. Roberts was listed as an orthopedic surgeon. She could find neither Patterson nor Morales.

A chill went down her spine. Patterson and Morales were probably residents. They were not in private practice and not listed in the yellow pages because, as residents, they were employees of Memorial Hospital. She'd bet on it.

Slow down, she told herself. Let's check all this out. First, I need to get the Discharge Note, she thought. For some reason the clerk had failed to include it. Then I need to find out if Patterson and Morales are residents. If they are, I wonder if Margaret knew that?

She picked up the phone and called the Medical Records clerk. When the woman answered, Consuela said, "This is Consuela Travis. You were kind enough to send me Joe Baxter's records a couple of weeks ago. Do you remember?"

"Yes," the woman answered.

"I just realized that the Discharge Note isn't here. Could you locate that and send it to me, please."

"It isn't there?"

"No, and I can certainly understand how you might have missed copying something. There's almost a thousand pages here."

"Well, I'll check and get back to you. Mrs Baxter did sign the release form, didn't she?"

"Yes, you have that on file."

"OK."

"Thank you."

When Consuela hung up, she sat for a minute thinking. Damn, this is getting strange.

She had agreed to look at the record so she could explain to Margaret why Joe had died. Should have been a relatively simple thing. Now she found herself confused and not a little suspicious.

Why was Boswell listed as the admitting doctor and therefore the presumed doctor in charge if he had rarely seen Joe? Maybe he had seen Joe but just hadn't bothered to write the notes in the Doctors Progress Reports. She knew that wasn't likely. Hospital procedure required doctors to write notes when they examined or treated a patient.

Maybe Boswell had just admitted Joe to the hospital but after the initial surgery had not been the doctor in charge and somehow the name of the actual doctor in charge had never been changed on Joe's identification card. She looked at the medical record again. At the top of every page of the record was an imprint, made from what appeared to be a plastic ID card.

The imprint said:

Baxter, Joseph L A2-441205 M 33 Episc Boswell S X-12 MD SCU2 321B

Consuela figured the A2-441205 was Joe's patient number. The M meant male, the 33 was Joe's age, the Episc probably stood for Episcopalian. She's check that with Margaret. Boswell was clear. What was the S? She looked in the telephone book again and saw his name was Sam Boswell. The S was his initial. The X-12 was probably his hospital doctor's number and MD was obviously for Medical Doctor. She was sure the SCU2 stood for Special Care Unit 2 and the 321D was probably Joe's bed number.

What was the significance of Boswell's name on Joe's ID card? Was he the doctor in charge or not? If he was, why hadn't he written more notes? If he wasn't in charge, who was?

Then Consuela realized that the Discharge Note, when she got it, would clear up some of the mystery. The doctor in charge had to write the Discharge Note. She could hardly wait to see who had written it. If it was Boswell, she had lots of questions!

The next day Consuela and Cynthia drove to San Elizario to see Margaret. They decided not to call before they went. If they were right, Margaret would just try to make some excuse not to see them if they called. They'd just arrive. They really wanted to get her out of the house, make her start seeing people.

When they parked in front of the farm house, a dog, madly wagging his tail and barking, bounded up to the car. Cynthia got out, leaned down and put her hand out to the dog. He sniffed and licked her hand. Cynthia squatted down and put her arms around the dog's neck. "Hey fella," she said, "What's up?" The dog licked her face.

Consuela laughed. Cynthia Hall Steelman was a sucker for any animal. Funny thing was, Consuela had never seen an animal that didn't love Cynthia.

The door to the house opened and Margaret stood there looking puzzled. When she saw it was Consuela and Cynthia, she smiled. "Barton," she said, "Leave Cynthia alone."

"Barton, old Buddy," said Cynthia, "the jiggs up. Your mamma says we've got to stop playing like this." She gave the dog a big hug and stood up.

Consuela and Cynthia walked to the house and Cynthia put her arms around Margaret. "I'm so sorry about Joe, Margaret, " she said.

Margaret hugged Cynthia and said, "Thank you." Consuela kissed Margaret and the three women stood there for a minute, holding each other.

"Now Margaret," said Cynthia, "Get your purse. We're going to Ysleta and feast at Carmen's."

Margaret had a momentary look of panic. Cynthia saw the look and said, "Lady, no excuses, no arguments! Fantastic enchiladas await! Pronto! Let's get going."

It was difficult to argue with Cynthia when she was determined and Margaret laughed and said, "OK."

They talked about a number of neutral topics on the ride. Margaret laughed when Consuela mentioned that her mother and father always talked about the "old road" and the cottonwood trees that used to arch over it. "Old timers in San Elizario still talk about it. Must have been something," said Margaret.

CHAPTER TWO

While they ate, Consuela waited for an opportunity to ask Margaret a few questions about Joe's doctors. Toward the end of the meal, Cynthia excused herself to go talk to someone she knew sitting across the room.

"Margaret, I want to ask you a few questions about Joe, OK?"

"Sure."

"Who was his doctor?"

"What do you mean? He had several doctors."

"Who was in charge? Was there an doctor in overall charge of Joe's care?"

"I would have to say Dr. Patterson. Why?"

"I was just curious. As you say, he had lots of doctors. Do you know whether Dr. Patterson was an attending physician or a resident?"

"What do you mean?"

"Well, a resident is a doctor still in training. Not yet in private practice. He's a staff doctor. An attending is a doctor in private practice who has hospital privileges, you know, can admit patients, can operate in the OR, things like that. Do you know which Dr. Patterson was?"

"An attending, I guess. I don't think he was in training," said Margaret with a frown on her face. "But, I really don't know. I never thought about it. I assumed he was a regular doctor."

"You weren't told he was a resident, if he was?"

"Absolutely not!"

"I'll check on it. By the way, what was Joe's religion?"

"Episcopalian."

"And how old was Joe?"

"Thirty three."

"OK. Did you talk to Dr. Sam Boswell while Joe was in the hospital?"

"I don't think so. Who's he?"

"He's a doctor who is an attending at Memorial. Sure you didn't talk to him? He's a surgeon."

"Connie, I may have. I can't remember. Perhaps toward the end I may have talked to him. Is he a tall guy with kind of gray hair?"

"I don't know," said Margaret. She felt her mind racing. Why was Boswell listed as the admitting doctor if Margaret couldn't even remember if she had ever talked to him?

Should she tell Margaret anything yet? Probably not. She wanted to be certain she knew what she was talking about. She still didn't understand why Joe had died. Be careful. Don't get Margaret upset until you know for sure what happened, she told herself.

"Connie, is something wrong? Do you know why Joe died?"

"Not yet, Margaret. I'm sure I will soon though. I'll call you or come see you as soon as I do."

That night Consuela asked Fred is she could ask him some general questions about the hospital.

"Is this about Joe Baxter?"

"Only in a general way. If any question bothers you, don't answer. OK?"

"OK."

"Do you know Dr. Patterson?"

"Randy Patterson? The surgeon?"

"Yes. Is he a resident or an attending?"

"A resident. He'll finish his residency this year, I think."

"What about Dr. Morales?"

"I don't know him but I know he is an orthopedic surgeon."

"Is he a resident or an attending?"

"I think he just became an attending. He's now in practice with Don Roberts."

"What does Sam Boswell look like?"

Fred laughed. "I can't imagine why you want to know, but he's tall, has gray hair. He's about 60 years old."

"Is a Discharge Note written on every patient?"

"Yep. Every patient admitted to the hospital has to have a Discharge Note written. Hospital regs."

"Who writes the Discharge Note?"

"The doctor."

"What if there are several doctors in charge?"

"The guy or gal in charge. Normally, that would be the admitting physician, but whoever had primary responsibility would file the Discharge Note."

"Is a resident ever the doctor in charge?"

"No way! As far as I know, an attending always admits a patient and remains the doctor in charge. I believe the hospital regulations require it, but I'm not sure. Certainly a resident might be very involved, may well see the patient more that the attending, but the person in charge is always an attending."

"There are other things I'd like to ask but I'm afraid it might make you uncomfortable. Can I get a copy of the hospital regulations?"

"I don't really know. Are you filing some kind of malpractice suit?"

"No. At least, I don't think so."

"You know what I think about malpractice cases!" said Fred beginning to frown. "Consuela, just because somebody dies sure as hell does not mean there was any malpractice!"

"Wait a minute. Don't get so riled up!" said Consuela, beginning to feel attacked. She felt her face flush. "I don't file cases frivolously, damn it! If I think there was malpractice, I would file. If I don't, I wouldn't."

"Are you going to file in this case?"

"I don't know."

"Well, damn it, I'm not going to talk to you again about any of this! You better be damn sure about what you're doing. Don't expect any help from me."

"Fine," said Consuela as she stood up and walked out of the room.

Their anger lasted through most of the evening. They talked very little during dinner. Fred thought about how much he despised malpractice cases and thought the overall rash of suits during the past decade had accomplished little to improve medicine. All that had been accomplished was to raise insurance rates to ludicrous levels and thus to increase the cost of medical care. Consuela thought to herself that if doctors would only police themselves there would be few cases of real malpractice. But doctors were notorious in their unwillingness to challenger another doctor.

Fred thanked Consuela for the dinner. Their kiss goodbye was perfunctory.

Well, she thought as she fell asleep that night, I hope the Discharge Note can clarify Joe's case. She wanted to be able to explain to Margaret why Joe had died. She didn't want to file a malpractice case. She didn't want the tension it would create with Fred.

Consuela received the Discharge Note two weeks later. She anxiously read the material. The note referred to Joe's initial problems, the paralysis that occurred and the infection. There was some detail about subsequent surgery, done in an attempt to locate the source of the systemic infection. The later surgery involved the stomach area around the gastrostomy tube.

Consuela hurriedly read the note until she came to the end. It was signed Sam Boswell, MD.

My God, thought Consuela. Sam Boswell. Boswell was the doctor in charge. And Margaret wasn't sure if she had ever talked to him! If

Boswell wrote the Discharge Note, that meant he was the doctor in charge and yet he hadn't written a single note in the Doctor's Progress report during the first two weeks after Joe's surgery. What the hell was going on?

Consuela felt a sudden chill: was it accidental that the hospital conveniently "forgot" to send the Discharge Note when they had copied Joe's entire medical record ? Not Likely!

She picked up the document and stared at Boswell's signature. Then she noticed the date. Her eyes bulged. It was dated last week. LAST WEEK. The Discharge Note had been written last week. No wonder the hospital hadn't sent it with the rest of Joe's records. They hadn't had it. Boswell hadn't written it until she asked for it. She did a quick calculation and realized it had been nine weeks since Joe died. Surely hospital regulations required that the Discharge Note be written "in a timely manner" or some such phrase. Surely nine weeks wasn't "timely."

Then she realized that if Boswell hadn't written it until she had specifically asked for it, he wrote it knowing a lawyer wanted to see it. Obviously he would be damned careful about what he wrote, smelling a possible malpractice case.

Why hadn't he written it when Joe died? "Oh...suppose he had," thought Consuela, "and the hospital didn't want her to see it and they substituted this for the original..."

Her mind began to race. . She stopped herself. "Slow down, girl'" she told herself. "Think carefully."

Then she realized that if they had substituted a second Discharge Note they certainly wouldn't have dated it last week. They would have dated it a short time after Joe's death.

OK. That meant Boswell simply hadn't written until last week. Why not? Short of asking him why, she didn't know how to find out. At some point, she would have to ask him.

Boswell's note was pretty vague about the paralysis. He just wrote that "after complaints of paralysis, the patient was found to have a displaced fracture at C6,7." That wasn't helpful. Had he had the fracture all along? Surely not or he would have been paralyzed from the beginning and he wasn't. So, why the sudden paralysis?

Boswell did write in some detail about the original surgery to repair the internal injuries and the later surgery after the paralysis when the infection became a problem.

Consuela carefully read the section about the second surgery. There was necrotic tissue. She knew that meant that the tissue had died. Boswell mentioned a perforation "of the anterior wall of the stomach." Why was there a hole in Joe's stomach?

She put the Discharge Note down and got Joe's medical records out. She looked again at the operating room notes for the initial surgery. The notes recorded that the liver had been repaired, a chest tube had been placed and a gastrostomy tube had been placed "on the antrum of the stomach."

Surely the "antrum" was the same as the "anterior wall of the stomach." She made a note to look it up to be sure.

Had the G-tube perforated the stomach? She saw that the G-tube had been stitched with "prolene sutures". If they had stitched the G-tube, had it slipped and cause the perforation? How could it slip if it had been properly placed and stitched? Apparently, it had been OK at first, but something had happened. And why was there necrotic tissue?

She made a note to look up "prolene". She assumed it was not the kind of suture that dissolved. You would want a non-dissolving suture material for holding a G-tube in place.

She put down the medical record. She was going to have to spend some time researching some of the medical terms. She saw a long Google session coming. She started a list of things she needed to look up.

She remembered something about the problem of healing, some notes about nurses working to keep the dressings dry because the infection wasn't healing. On a hunch, she picked up the Nurses Progress Report.

She found what she was looking for. Orelia Ortiz was the primary nurse involved in Joe's care. She found what Ortiz had written about the lack of healing. She now read very carefully. There was an entry written a couple of days before the surgical report mentioned the perforated stomach. Ortiz had written:

> "Dr Patterson discovered necrotic tissue around the G-tube with a pronounced lack of healing at the incision. First time the Vinke halo-brace removed. Changed dressing twice to insure dryness. Temp elevated all day. Purulent material draining from incision. No change in paralysis. Patient disoriented."

Consuela thought for a minute. Was there a connection between the Vinke brace and the slipped G-tube? How far down did the Vinke brace come? She knew the brace was a halo-like mechanism that had been placed on Joe's head after he became paralyzed. Margaret had told her about the brace. Did the bottom part come down to Joe's chest? Could it have touched the G-tube?

Was it significant that the Vinke brace had not been removed until then? She thought so since Orelia Ortiz had noted that it was the first time it had been removed and when it was removed Dr Patterson had discovered the necrotic tissue.

She was willing to bet that the brace had covered at least part of the G-tube incision, that for some reason the G-tube incision wasn't healing, had become infected, the infection grew worse and not until they removed the Vinke brace had they been able to see what the problem was.

She flipped back several pages in the Nurse's Progress Report to the days before the brace was removed. Sure enough, for five days before, Joe had an elevated temperature, a sign of infection.

What had they done about it? Consuela checked the medication record for those days. Morphine sulfate, Tylenol, Decadron and Valium. Tylenol she understood. Morphine sulfate was probably a morphine derivative for pain. I need to check that, she decided. She started a new list of drugs she would have to check in the Physicians Desk Reference. She had used it during previous cases and knew everyone called it the PDR and that it was now partially available online. What was Decadron? She did understand Valium.

Consuela began to think there might well be a malpractice case. There were lots of loose ends, much that she didn't understand. But things were becoming clearer. Should she tell Margaret anything yet? She couldn't be sure yet but she did need to tell Margaret something.

She called her and when Margaret answered the phone she said, "Hi, Margaret."

"Oh, Connie. How are you?"

"Fine. And you?"

"OK. Any information yet?"

"Margaret I am finding things that disturb me but I need to do a bit more research. Do you want to know what I have found so far or wait until I'm finished?"

"Connie, I want to know what you have found. I'm not surprised you've found things that disturb you. There was a <u>lot</u> that disturbed me about Joe's treatment! In a way, I'm relieved that you're disturbed. Means I wasn't crazy. When I tried to ask them questions, they just brushed me off. You know I've always been shy and it was difficult for me to question the doctors. Most of the time they barely spoke to me. When things got really bad, they spoke to me even less. They'd say things like, 'We've got to operate. Sign this.' When I tried to question them, I got only vague answers. The only person who ever really talked to me was Orelia Oritz, the nurse, but I could tell she was being careful about what she said sometimes."

Consuela could tell that Margaret was beginning to cry and said, "Margaret, I know this is difficult. Be strong."

"Connie, I'm trying. I've never said this to anyone but I don't believe for a minute that Joe should have died. I think they handled the case wrong. I want to talk to you in person. I want to file a law suit against them!"

Consuela was shocked by this outburst. "Margaret, there may or may not be a malpractice case. I don't know enough yet to be sure. I am beginning to think so, but I'm not yet sure."

"Well if there is, I want to sue."

"Don't be so quick to decide to sue. That is a long and emotionally horrifying road to start down."

"Do you mean you wouldn't represent me?"

"Margaret, of course, I would represent you if I thought there was a case here. Look, I'll do some research tomorrow. I'll probably go to the hospital library to check a couple of things. Why don't you come in Thursday and we'll talk."

"Good. I'll be there. What time?"

Consuela checked her calendar. "How about ten in the morning?"

"Fine. And, Connie, thanks."

The next day Consuela met Cynthia Steelman for lunch. They needed to discuss some final details for the bridal shower/luncheon that Cynthia was giving for Consuela the next week.

After they ordered, and had gone over the final details for the party, Cynthia said, "Guess who's coming to the party."

Consuela smiled and said, "Margaret Baxter?"

"How did you know?"

"Just a hunch. You know something Cyn, I think there's a real person inside that shy shell."

"God, Consuela, don't get carried away. Just because she's coming to the luncheon..."

"No, you ninny. I had a very interesting talk with her on the phone. She was not the kid who lived on "Old Maids Alley" in the dorm at Radford. She has asked me to look into Joe's death and I told her I had found some disturbing things. The minute I said that, she was a changed woman."

"In what way?"

"It was like some flood gate opened. She said she had thought Joe's treatment wasn't right, that when she asked the doctors about anything, they just brushed her off. The remarkable thing was, Margaret let me see her anger and resentment."

"Little mouse Margaret?"

"Yep, that little mouse may turn into a lion."

"I gotta see this. I've never seen Margaret show anger at anything in all these years. Good for her! What are you finding out about Joe's treatment?"

"I can't talk about it right now because I don't understand it all yet. In any case, it would be up to Margaret to tell you whatever she wanted. We may file a lawsuit."

"Oh, God. Fred will just love that," said Cynthia, looking very concerned.

"Bingo. I don't even want to think about how unhappy it would make him. It certainly would make his life difficult, being engaged to the Dragon Lady. You know how doctors stick together."

"Tell you what, though. I'm sure Fred would resent it, but if you've really got a case, he would be able to see that."

"From your mouth to God's ear."

"Are you going to tell him you may file suit?"

"At some point, obviously. I can't tell him anything now because I don't know yet. But I feel guilty running off with him to see architects and real estate people, knowing I may file suit against some doctors he knows and the hospital where he does his surgery. He's going to be hopping mad."

"How far will he hop?"

"Hop right out of the engagement? I don't think so. If he cancelled the wedding plans because I filed a legitimate malpractice claim, then that would say something about him that I wouldn't like. Better to find that out now."

"Jesus, girl. You don't think he would, do you?"

"No. I really don't. I certainly hope not. He's going to be mighty unhappy if it happens, but that's all."

"Have you had the closing on your land yet?"

"Yep and I'm excited by the plans the architects are drawing up."

"I gotta tell you, I'm jealous. You're house is going to be terrific. By the way, Fred got Jim so pumped up about the house that he's cutting stuff from magazines and saving it for Fred, you know, little ideas for the house. Jim's pushing for a big Jacuzzi so we can all soak away the strains of the day," said Cynthia, laughing.

"My mom and dad are doing the same thing!" Consuela said.

Cynthia looked at her watch and said, "Yipes, I've gotta get going. I've got a meeting at the Art Museum at one."

"Are you still working on renovating that space that houses your beloved Artemisia Gentileschi's painting?"

"Yep, we're almost done. The renovation should begin next month and we've made great arrangements to store the Gentileschi and the Titian safely and securely."

"Do the jockeys and trainers at Sunland Park know you're an art maven?"

Cynthia laughed loudly. "Hell no! If I said Artemisia Gentileschi or Titian they'd assume I was talking about some new horses! They don't even know I'm on the Board at the museum. Who knew those art history courses I took in college would stick with me the rest of my life. Great fun!"

"You remember that great trip we took to Houston to see the Frida Kahlo exhibit at the Houston Fine Arts? Now that was some exhibit!"

"It was. I thought you were overboard about Kahlo, but you were right. The best trip we took was to New York to see the Gentileschi exhibit at the Met."

Consuela laughed and said, "And we saw Liz Smith eating with Beverly Sills and Barbara Walters at Le Cirque. Great trip, I admit!"

They paid the bill and walked outside. Consuela hugged Cynthia and said, "OK, girlfriend, I've got to go and do some research for Margaret."

Consuela walked into the medical library at the hospital. It always made her a bit uncomfortable to do research in that library, particularly when the research might lead to a lawsuit against the hospital, but such research was allowed in public hospitals and the medical library had information Consuela wanted to check. Besides, the research might lead her to the conclusion that nothing had been all that wrong with Joe's treatment.

She decided to clear up the paralysis issue first. She had seen lots of new research in journals through a Google search, but she needed the basics. She walked over to a computer to access their on-line catalogue. She wrote down the names of some books about orthopedics and radiology. She asked the librarian for the books and when she got them, she sat down at a table and began to read.

After half an hour she knew one thing for certain: if a cervical spine injury was suspected, the X-rays must include the first <u>seven</u> vertebrae. Consuela was certain that the early X-rays had shown only the first five. She remembered the phrase "negative to C-5." Why hadn't the X-rays shown down to C-7?

She look again at the on-line catalogue and asked for four other books. Every book made clear that a cervical spine X-ray should show down to C-7. "I've gotcha," she thought. She made a note to check, to double check, that Joe's X-rays had only shown down to C-5. She felt sure she had the start of a case here.

But, she wondered, even if that's true, can we prove that lead to his paralysis? She again went through some of the books. She read for another twenty minutes. She was certain that Joe's records showed a displaced fracture at C-6,7. She would check. But it seemed clear that if they had known Joe had a fracture at C-6 they would have put him in a hard collar or brace so he couldn't turn his head.

When Joe had been admitted to the hospital he wasn't paralyzed. The paralysis hadn't occurred for several days. As she remembered the record: Joe had turned his head and the result was an instant paralysis. He'd had a soft collar on. Obviously, the doctors had been suspicious or they wouldn't have put the soft collar back on. She remembered all the notes by the nurses about numbness and bilateral weakness.

Since the original X-rays had not shown the standard first seven vertebrae, the prudent course of action would have been to put him in a hard collar or brace until they could do another X-ray that showed down to C-7.

"Wait a minute," she thought. "So I can show negligence about the paralysis. That didn't kill him. He died from systemic infection. Unless I can show some connection between the paralysis and the infection, I can't show that this negligence killed him."

She sat thinking for several minutes. She knew that paralysis didn't cause infection. She felt discouraged.

She might be able to get Margaret some settlement on the paralysis. God knows, Margaret needed the money. She also needed a sense of justification that she had been right in being troubled about Joe's treatment.

But she knew she couldn't get a large settlement because they could show they were aggressively treating him and that he might have recovered. Besides, it was the infection, not the paralysis, that had killed him.

Consuela then checked the computer terminal again and checked out several books on infections and she was not encouraged by what she read. Joe had no doubt gotten a staph infection in the hospital. Margaret quickly realized, however, that she couldn't prove negligence just because he became infected in the hospital. Virtually all hospitals had staph germs and she knew that as long as the hospital could show they had followed standard procedures of sanitation and sterilization they weren't negligent.

Margaret was pretty sure the hospital was careful about sanitation. It was a good hospital. "Ironic," she thought. "I do think Memorial is a good hospital. I think they goofed badly somewhere in Joe's care, but if I got sick, I'd want to come here."

Consuela knew that before she would file a suit the mistakes they made had to be egregious. Not just mistakes. Big mistakes. Bad mistakes. Willful mistakes.

She knew she hadn't yet found such mistakes. There certainly seemed to be culpability about the paralysis. But that hadn't killed Joe.

Consuela glanced down at her watch and saw that it was almost four. She stretched and tried to loosen the kinks in her back. She looked down at her list of questions and saw that she still needed information about the Vinke brace so she could see if it went down low enough to touch the G-tube.

She looked at the index of a recently published orthopedic book and found an entry about Vinke braces. She turned to the pages indicated. The first picture showed the brace. Mean looking thing, she thought. She turned the page and saw a picture of the brace on a patient.

Her heart leaped. The bottom of the brace came down below the chest.

"My God," she thought. "The thing could easily have covered some of the G-tube incision! If they never removed the brace, an infection could have started there and they wouldn't have seen it! No wonder Orelia Ortiz had noted that was the first time the brace had been removed and that Dr. Peterson had then <u>discovered</u> the infection. The nurse knew!"

She started reading the text about the Vinke brace. She hurried through the gruesome details about screwing the halo-like apparatus into the patient's skull. Poor Joe! She was searching for some measurements for the bottom part of the brace, the part that came down below the chest.

She had to look in two more books before she found what she was looking for. The brace came in several sizes. Joe was big. She needed to Xerox those pages to get the measurements for the two biggest sizes. She'd bet anything that it would show it covered the top of the G-Tube incision. Orelia Ortiz's notes certainly implied that. She'd have to look at Joe's record and get some measurements of where the G-tube was exactly. If she couldn't find that, she'd damn sure find out at a deposition whether the bottom of the brace covered some of the G-tube incision.

At a deposition. She had just thought about a deposition. She realized she was pretty certain that she might have found the Big Mistake, the Bad Mistake, the Willful Mistake and that she might well file a malpractice suit. She also realized she needed to do more research. She wouldn't serve Margaret well until she was certain. She still had to research the medications.

She picked up the stack of books without paper markers and gave them back to the librarian and took the ones with paper markers over to the Xerox machine. She fed the machine $5 and started xeroxing.

She looked out the window as the machine made the copies. The sun was beginning to get low in the sky, with sunlight and clouds dappling the mountain.

She knew she had lots more work to do. But she felt she had found the key.

She suddenly thought about Fred. "Oh God," she thought. "This is going to be damn difficult."

Chapter Three
The Domino Effect

The next morning before she went to the office, Consuela called her father. "Hey Pops," she said, "How are you and Mom?"

"Fine, fit and happy!" he answered. "What about you and Fred?"

"Fine...at the moment. But Dad, I am getting close to thinking I should file a malpractice suit for Margaret Baxter. I need to ask you a couple of things. Do you know Sam Boswell?"

"The surgeon? Of course. Really nice guy. Used to play golf with him at the country club before he switched to the Coronado Country Club. Why? Is he involved in this thing?"

"He is listed as the Admitting Doctor on the records but weeks went by without him signing the Doctor's Progress report."

"That's strange. Perhaps there's an explanation. Be careful. Well, I know you'll be careful, but Sam has done a lot for this community. Do like I taught ya gal, check everything, double check."

"That's what I'm doing. But I need to go over some stuff with you. When are you going to come in to the office?"

"How about Tuesday?"

"Great. Give mother my love."

That night she and Fred went to the Steelman's for dinner. Consuela had to concentrate to keep her mind off Joe Baxter. She felt awkward not telling Fred anything. She had never before kept things from him, but she wasn't positive what she was going to do about the Baxter case and she didn't want to borrow trouble.

She took a sip of her gin and tonic and tried to listen to the conversation. She heard Fred say, "Hey Cyn, what's the name of that horse you love so much?"

"Which one?" said Cynthia, laughing.

"You mean Ready to Run?" asked Jim, laughing. "I'm thinking about asking Consuela to file suit against that horse for alienation of affection."

They laughed and Cynthia said, "I'll have you know Ready to Run is without doubt the class horse at Sunland Park! And I do give him big, smoochy kisses every day!"

"Well, when are we going to see this big wonder horse at work?" asked Consuela.

"Well, Miss Priss, it just so happens he's going to win the big stakes race on Sunday! If ya wanna make a little money..."

"Cynthia, you're incorrigible! How much are you going to bet?"

"Lady, this is a sure thing! I'm putting $500 on his nose. Come see. I'll win!"

"Consuela, what do you say," asked Fred. "Can we pass up this deal?"

"Wouldn't miss it!" said Consuela.

"God, I'm glad you're coming," said Jim, putting his arm around Cynthia. "When she has a horse in the lead heading for the finish, she starts pounding me! You can protect me."

During dinner they made plans to attend the early service at St Clement's Episcopal Church, then meet at the Steelman's and go to brunch, go to the new property that Fred and Consuela had bought and then on to the races.

That night as Consuela was falling asleep she thought about the fun they'd have on Sunday. But she was worried. By Sunday she would probably know if she was going to file the malpractice suit. That might put a strain on things. First thing in the morning, she reminded herself, she needed to check Joe's medical record to be certain that the initial X-rays had shown down to C5 and not to C7.

The next morning when she got to the office, Consuela called her dad at the ranch.

"Hi Pops. How are you?"

"Fine. It's a beautiful morning! Your mom and I sat out front and watched the fish jumping in the lake. Gonna run into Marfa and get a few groceries. What's up?"

"Just want to be sure you will you be in the office on Tuesday?"

"That's the plan. You sound a bit nervous. Want me to be there Monday?"

"No, Tuesday will be fine. I am very close to filing the malpractice suit and there are some things I've got to check before I see you and then go over the whole thing with you. OK? And Pops, I am a bit nervous."

"Certainly isn't going to be easy on Fred, is it. Anything I can do to help you with that?"

"No. I'll just have to deal with it if I do file the suit. But I will need your hard-headed appraisal on Tuesday. OK?"

"I'll give you my best."

"Great, I'll have Marge block out the afternoon for us. And Dad, thanks."

Consuela then got out Joe's records and started checking. She was right: the initial X-rays had shown down only to C-5. They had not shown down to C-7. <u>After</u> the paralysis, the X-rays had shown down to C-7.

She was reading the record when Marge knocked on the door, opened it and said, "Margaret is here."

"Fine. Send her in."

Marge brought Margaret in and sat a tray with coffee down on the table. Consuela got up and hugged Margaret. They talked for a minute and then Consuela said, "Margaret I want to ask you some questions first and then I'll tell you what I found. OK?"

"OK."

"How far down did that halo-brace come down on Joe's chest?"

"Below his chest. Kind of to the top of his stomach."

"Do you remember if it came down as low as the Gastric tube? Remember the tube they used to feed Joe?"

"Yes. And yes it came down that low. At least it touched it. I remember Orelia cleaning Joe and it worried me because the brace was touching the tube. I thought it might be painful for Joe."

"OK. Now think carefully. Did you ever talk to Dr. Boswell?"

"Connie, I honestly can't remember. I may have. If I did talk to him it was only a couple of times. I talked to lots of doctors. He doesn't stand out."

"Did you know that Dr. Boswell was the doctor in charge of Joe's care?"

"Absolutely not! I thought Dr. Patterson was. Was Dr. Boswell in charge?" Margaret began to show her anger, her cheeks were flushed. She gritted her teeth. "Why didn't I know that? Why didn't he take care of Joe? He was never around!"

"And you didn't know that Dr. Patterson was a resident, not an attending?"

"I would have insisted on a regular doctor. I liked Dr. Patterson most of the time, but I would have insisted on someone with more experience."

"What exactly did they tell you when Joe became paralyzed?"

"Just that Joe had turned his head and caused a fracture which had left him paralyzed. They seem to imply that it was Joe's fault." Margaret's anger was rising. "They implied it was all Joe's fault for turning his head."

"Did they ever talk to you about his early X-rays? Any conversation about C-5, or not being able to see down to the seventh cervical vertebrae?"

"No. I don't know what you're talking about. After he was paralyzed, I do remember Dr. Morales telling me he had a fracture."

"What did they tell you about putting on the soft collar?"

"You mean the Vinke?"

"No, the soft collar that they put on him a few days before the paralysis."

"I think they said it would make him more comfortable."

"Did they tell you that Joe should not turn his head or anything?"

"No. Just that he would be more comfortable."

"OK. Did they say anything about Joe possibly recovering from the paralysis? Might just be temporary?"

"Yes. They said they were giving him steroids to reduce the swelling. That and the brace might result in some movement returning."

"Did he regain any movement before he died?"

"Some. At first, he had trouble moving his arms. That got OK. But he could never move his legs. Nothing below his chest."

"What did they tell you about his infection?"

"Just that he had an infection. They did lots of tests to find out what kind of infection and where it was located. They did some surgery to find the infection."

"And what did they tell you after the surgery?"

"They said they thought the infection had started in his stomach but that it had spread throughout his body."

"Where in the stomach?"

"They didn't say. I asked, but they never did say. They seemed irritated that I wanted to know more than just 'his stomach'. Frankly, they intimidated me Connie."

Margaret started to cry. Consuela got up and put her arms around Margaret, letting her cry and trying to offer comfort."

Finally, Margaret looked up. She wiped her eyes with Kleenex. She looked Consuela straight in the eye and said, "I am haunted because I let them intimidate me. Joe deserved better from me. If I had been more insistent, stronger, I might have found out more and been able to help

Joe. I have promised myself, sworn to God, that I will never be intimidated again! Never!"

"Good, " said Consuela softly. "Good Margaret. You've got more strength than you know. You're going to have to be really strong now because I am going to tell you what I found."

Margaret nodded her head. She listened intently as Consuela told her everything, what she had found and what she still needed to check. Consuela expected more tears but instead Margaret got more angry and determined. She clenched her teeth and Consuela could see the strong jaw line.

"Consuela, can we file a malpractice suit?"

Consuela was first struck by the fact that Margaret had called her Consuela and not Connie. That was one of the few times she'd done that. Most people called her Connie, but the strong people she loved, her mom and dad, Fred, Cynthia and Jim all called her Consuela. She thought it was a good sign that Margaret had called her Consuela.

"Margaret, I want to do a little more research to be sure. But I think we probably do have a case. I want to consult my dad about a couple of things. When I am positive, I'll tell you. But even that won't mean we should go ahead and file. Filing such a case will take an emotional toll. It will be very difficult for you." said Consuela.

"I'm not sure I would be able to pay you much," said Margaret.

"If we go ahead, let me tell you how the fees would work. You would have to pay for certain expenses that I would incur, things like having Marge type documents and Xerox, consultation with a medical expert, and for some of the hours I spend preparing the case. Those costs could add up to $10,000. This is standard practice in such cases. But nothing else. If we win the case, I would take one third of the settlement and you would get two thirds. That is also the standard practice. So we've both got to be sure we want to proceed. You've got to see about being able to pay the billable expenses and I've got to be pretty certain we'll win because this case would take most of my time for several months."

Margaret thought for a minute and said, "I believe I can come up with the $10,000. I'll do it even if I have to sell the farm. Let's sue the bastards!"

Consuela laughed and said, "We'll know shortly."

Margaret said, "What do I owe you for the work you've already done?"

"Now, that part isn't standard practice. I've done this out of friendship. But, if we go ahead, the bills will mount."

Margaret smiled and said, "I'm grateful."
"So, how about lunch?"
"Great. Where shall we go?"
"How about Jaxon's?"
"Good. I've never been there and I'd like to try it."
Consuela smiled and thought to herself that the old Margaret would have begged off about going to lunch. Consuela liked the new Margaret better.

Consuela and Fred and the Steelman's attended the early service at St Clement's and then went to the Steelman's house for Bloody Marys. They raised their glasses in a toast to Ready to Run. The four friends then went to the Hacienda restaurant for breakfast.

The Hacienda was a very old adobe building, built on the banks of the Rio Grande river in the 1800's. The past 100 years or so it had housed a restaurant that was commonly agreed by all to have the very best chili con queso in the world. It was served in a large bowl, and instead of a gooey, hydrogenated mess, this chili con queso was served in a broth with large chunks of white cheese barely melting, large pieces of roasted and peeled, fresh Hatch green chili, barely softened chopped onion, a bit of garlic and some chopped fresh tomatoes. A plate of freshly made flour tortillas accompanied the bowl.

Jim ordered a large bowl for the four of them to share. Consuela and Cynthia ordered huevos rancheros and Jim and Fred ordered chorizo and scrambled eggs.

As they ate in one of the thick-walled adobe rooms, sunlight streamed in through the windows. It was already hot outside but the adobe kept the interior cool.

When they finished eating Fred and Jim went to check out the wall structure in another part of the building, hoping to get some ideas for Fred's and Consuela's house. Cynthia and Consuela sat and drank some coffee and talked.

Cynthia was running high on energy because of her excitement about Ready to Run. She was convinced he was going to win. She explained the race strategy that she and the trainer had devised: go out fast, hang in just behind the leaders and move when they made the turn for home.

"Why not go for the lead to begin with?" asked Consuela.

"Hell no, let some other horse wear himself out! We'll hang back and rest. Just gotta stay close enough to make our move. When the leaders begin to tire out, we'll be fresh. Ready to Run likes to finish strong. Good at pacing himself. This is one smart horse, girlfriend. He understands the point is to cross the finish line first. I swear he does!"

"Don't all horses understand that?"

"Not by a long shot," said Cynthia. "I've had lots of horses that just love to run. Just love it! But they want to boom out of the gate and run as fast as they can. Problem is they can't keep it up and so the jockey has to fight them the whole way, trying to pace them so they'll have something left at the finish. You can't do well if you're having to fight the horse the whole way."

"Are you really going to bet $500?"

"Damn straight. You better get something down on him too!"

"OK. OK. I'll bet a $15 combine, " said Consuela, laughing.

"Chicken!" said Cynthia, joining the laughter.

They gathered up their purses, getting ready to leave. "I wonder if we're going to have to find the boys," said Consuela..

"Hey, I meant to ask you. Are you going to file a suit for Margaret?"

"I'm not sure yet. It looks more and more likely."

"Have you said anything to Fred?"

"No. And I dread it. I don't want to say anything until I'm sure."

"Good luck."

They drove in their cars to see the land that Fred and Consuela had bought. They walked through the trees, mainly pecan and a few pear trees. Jim and Fred discussed the best orientation for the house while Cynthia and Consuela looked carefully to see how many of the trees could be saved when the house was built.

Finally, they drove to the race track. Cynthia and Jim went directly to their barn to check Ready to Run. Consuela and Fred went to the Clubhouse and waited in the Steelman's box.

During the afternoon they each studied the Daily Racing Form and made occasional small bets. Before the eighth race they all went to the paddock to watch Ready to Run get saddled.

The horse was gleaming in the bright sunshine and although he was very alert, he stayed calm. His rich, dark brown body and the jet black of his tail and mane were perfectly brushed. Jim and Fred and Consuela stayed on the outside of the paddock as Cynthia went in to the stall where Ready to Run was waiting. She and the trainer, Bobby Tanner, chatted quietly for a few minutes. Bobby threw the saddle and racing blanket over his back and cinched the strap. Cynthia was hugging the horse's neck and whispering to him when the jockey, Berto Lopez, walked up. Bobby talked to Berto about the strategy for the race, then boosted him up onto the saddle. They could hear the trumpet in the distance, calling the horses to the track.

As they walked back to the Clubhouse, Cynthia watched the horses warming up on the far side of the track. She smiled, pleased with the way Ready to Run was moving.

"OK, sports fans. The time is now. Get your money down," said Cynthia as she handed Jim $500. "On the nose, sweetheart. He's gonna do it!"

Consuela and Fred looked at each other and laughed. Fred said, "Consuela, Cynthia will be impossible to live with if she wins a bundle and we don't. What do you say? How about $25 on the nose?"

"What are the odds?" asked Consuela, looking at the tote board. Ready to Run was at 9 to 5, the favorite.

"I hate to bet the favorite," she said, grinning at Cynthia.

"Dummy, there are reasons why the favorite is the favorite. If it makes you happy, bet on number 2. He's at 50 to 1," replied Cynthia, grinning.

"OK, Fred. Do it. $25 ...on Ready to Run to win."

When Jim and Fred returned to the box, Fred was grinning. They all stood as the horses were loaded into the starting gate. Cynthia watched carefully through binoculars.

"They're off!" boomed the announcer over the public address system. "Going into the first turn, it's Foxy Baby, followed by Gambler's Pride and Ready to Run."

They watched as the horses made the first turn and started down the back stretch, stringing out in a long line. Ready to Run dropped back to fourth. Cynthia could see Berto pulling back on the reins as they approached the final turn.

"Perfect!" shouted Cynthia, watching through the binoculars.

The announcer continued his commentary over the public address system, "Turning for home, it's Foxy Baby still in front by half a length. Margo's Mark is next, followed by Ready to Run and Gambler's Pride. Now Ready to Run is coming through horses. He's passing Margo's Mark. Ready to Run is neck and neck with Foxy Baby."

Cynthia put down the binoculars and started pounding Jim's arm. "Come on horse. That's it. Do it!"

Consuela and Fred were also jumping up and down as Ready to Run passed Foxy Baby and took the lead. The jockey, Berto Lopez, had popped the horse once at the head of the stretch, the signal that it was time to run. He hadn't hit him again.

Jim picked up Cynthia and twirled her around as Ready to Run crossed the finish line a full two lengths ahead.

"Hot Damn," shouted Cynthia. "Hot Damn!"

"Look at this! Look at this!" Fred shouted to the group. He held up a $100 win ticket on Ready to Run. They all laughed and cheered. "I decided, if Cynthia was so damn sure, we'd go whole hog. I didn't want to listen to the I told you so's!"

"You sneak," laughed Consuela. "Would you have told me if we'd lost?"

"Sure, I'd have wanted your $50 share"

They rushed out of the Clubhouse and down to the Winner's Circle. When the horse entered the circle he was breathing heavily but he still pranced, full of energy. They all stood proudly by the horse and the track photographer snapped the picture. Cynthia yelled to him that she wanted a dozen prints.

Cynthia told them she had talked to Billy Crews and that he had put aside a 1989 bottle of Petrus Pomerol Bordeaux since she was sure she would win and they'd have it with some fine steak for dinner. They all loved to eat at Billy Crews. The wine was fabulous and they were an exuberant group.

On Monday morning, Consuela and Marge went over the calendar for the week. "Is your dad coming in tomorrow?"

"Far as I know."

"OK. I'll tell George Bradley he can see Bill at 10:00. How long should that meeting take?"

"Hmm. That's about the export license thing, isn't it? Not long. Dad told me he got that settled. Don't book anything for him after three. I need to have a long talk with him about the Baxter case."

"OK. How about this afternoon for you? The Howell's can see you this afternoon or on Wednesday. They prefer Wednesday."

"Tell them Wednesday. I've got to finish doing some research on the Baxter case. I may have to go back to the hospital library."

"OK. I'll have the Walker settlement ready for you this morning. Anything else?"

"Nope. Thanks Marge."

That afternoon Consuela started looking up the drugs Joe had been given. She decided to do a quick search first on the shortened Physician's Desk Reference, the PDR, that was available on the Nurse's web site. She could go over to the medical library later and xerox the full entry in the PDR if she found anything important.

She started with morphine sulfate. It was for pain, as she had guessed. Certainly seemed OK as Joe had been in a great deal of pain.

Next she looked up Decadron. It was a form of dexamethasone, an adrenocortical steroid. She read that it was used for symptomatic relief of inflammation, including swelling, among many other things. If they were using it to reduce swelling, it made sense. They were no doubt trying to reduce the swelling around the cervical spine to see if the paralysis would go away.

She made a few notes about the usual dosage, intending to check if Joe's doses were typical.

Then she started to read the section labeled "Contraindications." Only two things were listed: Systemic fungal infection. Hypersensitivity to any component of this product.

Consuela gasped. Decadron was contraindicated if there was systemic fungal infection. Joe died from a systemic infection. Was it fungal, she wondered.

She quickly went to the Merck Manual online. Bless them for putting the whole manual online, she thought. She typed in "systemic infection". She quickly found "Systemic Candidiasis". She read that Candida are organisms that "colonize the normal GI tract and sometimes the skin."

Then her eyes found the sentence that took her breath away:

> Infections due to Candida account for about 80% of all major systemic fungal infections.

"Bingo!" she shouted. She felt a chill run down her spine. This is it! Joe died of a systemic infection that Decadron had masked and was flatly contraindicated if there was a fungal infection.

Marge appeared in the doorway, having heard Consuela shout. "What's up?"

She asked.

"Marge, we've got a case. Go downstairs right now to that bookstore in the lobby and buy the latest edition of the PDR, you know, The

Physicians Desk Reference. If they don't have it, go down the street to that big bookstore."

Marge grinned as she stopped by her desk to pick up the law firm's Visa card. She loved to see Consuela this excited. Reminded her of Consuela's dad, Bill.

Marge returned ten minutes later with the book. Consulea was making notes on a legal pad. Marge handed her the book. Consuela thanked her and quickly opened the book to Decadron.

She read the article, seeing it was pretty much the same as what she had read online. But there was an additional section labeled "WARNINGS". The section was more than a page long but she read slowly and carefully:

> Corticosteroids may exacerbate systemic fungal infections and therefore should not be used in the presence of such infections. Corticosteroids may mask some signs of infection, and new infections may appear during their use. There may be decreased resistance and inability to localize infection when corticosteroids are used.

Consuela felt her heart pounding. "My God," she thought. "My god, poor Joe." She continued reading about the contraindications of the use of Decadron. In the section labeled "PRECAUTIONS" she read that Decadron would "impair wound healing."

Consuela closed the book. She took a deep breath. This was it: The Big Mistake, The Bad Mistake, The Willful Mistake. She had a case.

She got a fresh legal pad and wrote:
1. Joe admitted with multiple trauma, including a cut on the forehead. The cut had alerted the paramedics to put a soft collar around Joe's neck because of the possibility of a cervical spine injury.
2. The X-rays taken in the emergency room had failed to picture the cervical spine down to C-7, the standard. They had shown only to C-5.
3. During the surgery, a Gastric tube had been placed at the top of Joe's stomach.
4. After the emergency surgery, no collar had been placed around Joe's neck despite the lack of information about the full cervical spine. No additional X-rays were ordered.

5. Joe complained about numbness and had a weak bilateral hand grasp, signs of a cervical spine injury. Several days later a <u>soft</u> collar had been placed around his neck. The new X-rays still showed only to C-5.
6. Without the hard collar or brace, Joe could turn his head. He did and was suddenly paralyzed. X-rays were then ordered and showed a displaced fracture at C-6. The sixth cervical vertebrae had no doubt been fractured all along, causing the numbness and weak bilateral hand grasp. When he turned his head, the fracture had been displaced, riding up over the seventh vertebrae.
7. The orthopedic doctors had put Joe in traction with the Vinke brace, trying to pull the vertebrae back into alignment. They also gave him steroids, the Decadron, to reduce the swelling.
8. The Vinke brace covered the top of the G-tube incision and the Decadron impaired Joe's ability to fight the infection which developed at the top of the G-tube. Because they couldn't see the top of the G-tube incision, they didn't know it was infected. The result was a systemic fungal infection because the steroids blocked the body's ability to localize infection.
9. ALL these problems were compounded because no single doctor was in charge.

Boswell was supposed to be, but wasn't. The orthopods were just concerned about the bones. Boswell should have seen what effects the steroids would have on the surgical sites but he wasn't around. Patterson was around but he couldn't see the top of the gastric tube incision and he was a resident and no doubt loaded with patients.

Consuela put down her pen. She knew she had the outline of her case and it was strong. There might be some changes, but the essentials were there. It was a classic domino case, one thing led inevitably to another.

She called her dad. There was no answer at the ranch. She called his cell phone and got him. "Dad, are you on your way to El Paso?"

"Yep. I've got that meeting in the morning with George Bradley and your mom has a meeting at St. Clement's."

"Dad, I've got to see you this afternoon or tonight. Really important."

"Sure. Can you meet me at the house at three this afternoon?"

"Yep. Thanks Pops."

Consuela looked at her Rolodex and called Dr. Barnard Landis in Boston. She had used him several years ago in a medical case. He had taught her a great deal and was able to explain why she should avoid some issues. He advised her not to file suit. She trusted him. She briefly outlined the Baxter case to him and he agreed to look at the file.

She told Marge to xerox the entire file and send it to him.

Consuela called Margaret and told her she needed to see her and asked if she could come in tomorrow morning. She had to explain the case and be certain Margaret wanted to pursue it and was ready for the deep emotional toll it would take. Margaret said she would be there.

And, Consuela thought, I'm going to have to talk with Fred.

Chapter Four
Final Answers

Consuela and her father spent three hours talking about what she had discovered. Bill Travis listened carefully and with the appropriate skepticism, a skepticism that had grown less and less as she explained the record and showed him key documents.

Finally, Bill said, "Consuela, you've got a case. Superb work! Do you think Margaret will want to go forward? Can she afford the up-front costs?"

"I think she will want to sue. I've told her that the up-front costs may be as high as $10,000. She said she would find a way if I thought we had a case. I'm seeing her in the morning."

"Good. Here's something I want you to think about. When you take the pre-trial deposition, I want you to consider doing them in a different way."

"What do you mean?"

"You know that we always try to elicit information without giving away much of our case. We save the good stuff for trial, don't want them to know everything. But Texas law requires we file an expert's opinion within 90 days of filing a medical malpractice suit. If we can get them to agree to a deposition earlier, we can hit them hard because I also think they will not have put the facts together. They will come to the deposition convinced they acted heroically, that this is some junk malpractice suite."

"I agree."

" I think you are absolutely right that each set of doctors just paid attention to the stuff that concerned them. Obviously Sam Boswell was paying almost no attention and he was the one who should have been putting this together. He was the doctor in charge. By the way, how much did he bill the Baxter's for his care?"

"My God, I hadn't thought about that! Since he was the Admitting Doctor, his office would have billed the Baxter's for the surgery and the additional care. Margaret did not even recognize his name. I'll ask her to be sure, but I'll bet his office didn't send any bills because he truly forgot he was supposed to be the doctor in charge and never told his office. That will be additional proof of what we know happened in this case!"

"Yes indeed. Be sure to ask her tomorrow. By the way, Paul Morales, you know the doctor who worked with the chief orthopedic surgeon. He has the worst handwriting I have ever seen. That's what took me so long in trying to read the record. It is truly illegible and I'll bet you the other doctors can't read it either."

"I agree."

"Well, in any case, I don't think they've put the case together and I'll bet they will be shocked when you file suit. They will be outraged. They'll insist to their attorneys that they worked heroically and did nothing wrong. I'm sure they really don't think they did anything wrong. Their attorneys are likely to believe them because these are some of the best doctors around, some big guns with great reputations and they will seem truthful."

"Dad, I'm beginning to see where you're going with this."

"Schedule the depositions for late afternoon, say four o'clock, and I'll bet you all the doctors and lawyers involved will show up for the first depositions, even those who aren't scheduled to be deposed until the next day. They'll want to show solidarity and want to see what a weak case you've got. Their lawyers will encourage them to attend so they'll be ready the next day to deal with you. So, baby girl, what would be the advantage of revealing most of your case at the deposition instead of waiting for the trial?"

Consuela began to nod her head and smile, "If my questions to the first couple of people reveal the extent of our case, they may all get <u>really</u> nervous and want to settle. I believe I can get the doctors and attorneys to see the validity of our case. I'll make sure to make enough copies of the parts of the record I want to use at the depositions, all the key documents, so the lawyers can have serious discussions with their clients about the need to settle. They sure as hell wouldn't want this stuff to come out in a public trial."

"Exactly," said Bill. "And Consuela, if we can get them to settle it will be better for Margaret. She won't have to go through the agony of a public trial and it will cost her a whole lot less money. And, frankly, I'm not interested in humiliating these doctors or the hospital. That's a great hospital and the doctors I know are really good doctors and serve this community well. They just goofed badly, fatally, in this case."

"Dad, do you want to do the deposition with me?"

Chapter Four

"Hell no, girl! You go in there alone, alone against a roomful of lawyers. They'll be cocky at first, thinking this will be a boring deposition, a waste of their time. They'll probably try to intimidate you. And their lawyers will point out to each other that we're in general practice, not specialists in medical malpractice, and probably don't know what we're doing."

Consuela laughed and nodded in agreement. Bill grinned and said, "Of course, if we go to trial, I'll sure as hell be sitting next to you as co-counsel!"

"And Dad I do need to talk to a medical expert. I had Marge send the records to Dr. Landis at Harvard. You remember him? He helped us five years ago on the Garcia's medical malpractice case, advised us not to file. I called him and he said he'd take a look. Should we wait to file until we've heard from him?"

"I guess so. We've got to file his written opinion within 90 days of filing the lawsuit. We do need him to affirm what we think. Just talk to him. We can wait on a written report until we see if they'll agree to an early deposition. Might be able to save Margaret some money. When do you expect to hear from him?"

"He said a conference he was scheduled to attend had been changed and so he thought he could do it this weekend. How about that!"

"Blessings from God, kiddo. How much will he charge?"

"He said between $2,000 and $3,000. Two thousand if he just talks to me and $3,000 if he has to write it up. If we go to trial, it will be an additional $5,000 to testify."

"Let's see if we can get by on $2,000. I'm convinced he'll agree with your assessment and I do believe we can stop this whole thing at a early deposition."

"OK. Let's see what Margaret decides. And help me decide whom I should depose first and second."

"I'll think about it. When are you going to tell Fred? That's going to be tough, I know."

"I'm going to call him and ask him to come over for dinner Friday night. I'm just going to tell him it looks like we'll file the malpractice suit but it isn't yet certain. I feel I ought to at least tell him that much. I'm certainly not going to discuss the particulars of the case with him. I don't look forward to it, I can tell you that."

Just then Maria Travis came into the den and said, "Mi hija, I've got dinner almost ready. I fixed that chicken you like, you know the roasted chicken with lemons and marjoram. Just let me know when you two are ready."

Bill and Consuela grinned and said, "We're ready!"

Margaret arrived at Consuela's office promptly at nine the next morning. Marge took her into Consuela's office and brought them coffee. They sat around a small table and after exchanging some small talk, Consuela said, "Margaret, I want to tell you why Joe died. Are you sure you want to hear?"

"Absolutely" answered Margaret.

"First, I want to ask you about the medical bills. From whom did you get bills for Joe's care?"

"From the hospital and from Doctors Morales and Roberts. The insurance has paid most of those bills."

"Did you get any bills from Dr. Sam Boswell?"

"I don't think so."

"Will you check your records when you go home?"

"Sure. I told you before that I'm not sure I even remember who he is. I think he talked to me after Joe was paralyzed, before they did the second surgery. Did he do the second surgery?"

"Yes. And the initial surgery the day Joe was brought to the hospital."

"Were his bills included in the bills from the hospital?"

"He is an attending so the bill should have come from his office. In any case, let me now tell you why Joe died."

Consuela spent two hours going over the medical records, carefully explaining what happened. Margaret listened intently and asked few questions. Consuela told her she had sent a copy of her records to Dr. Barnard Landis at Harvard so she could be certain that her conclusions were valid.

When Consuela indicated that she had finished, Margaret said, "Consuela, I knew something wasn't right. I knew it. Now it all makes sense to me and I am truly grateful to you for discovering the truth. So many things make sense to me now, things I didn't understand and that continued to bother me. To haunt me, really," Margaret said as tears rolled down her cheek. "But now I am as angry as I am sad."

"I understand."

"Consuela, I want to sue. Joe shouldn't have died and I owe him that. I also owe myself that. I have promised myself never again to be intimidated, to let people walk over me. I feel truly guilty about Joe. I feel I should have done more."

"Margaret, do not feel guilty. You weren't in charge of Joe's care. You don't have a medical background. You did what we all do: you trusted the doctors and the hospital. One of the things we can all learn from this is that we have a right to ask questions and insist on straight, clear answers. Don't feel guilty. Few of us learn that lesson when it comes to dealing with doctors."

Margaret shook her head in disagreement. She told Consuela that she was a stronger person than she had ever been but she was not entirely free of guilt. She should have done more. She said she still had to deal with the grief, the loneliness, the anguish she felt every morning when she woke up and realized Joe wasn't there, the tears she shed when she hugged big dog Barton who still seemed to look for Joe when he heard a pick-up truck. "But," she added, "I am also filled with anger and resentment at the doctors. I want to sue them, to show them they were wrong and they can't ignore me anymore!"

"I agree. I will almost certainly file the malpractice suit. I do want to wait until I talk to Dr. Landis, just to be sure."

"The Harvard doctor?"

"Yes. Then it will take me a few days to write the documents and get everything in order and decide whom to include in the suit. And Margaret, you need to face the fact that some people will be very angry that you are filing a malpractice case. You will be accused of trying to make money off Joe's death. You will be accused of being ungrateful to a group of doctors who did their best for Joe."

Margaret looked shocked. She felt hurt and humiliated that anyone would think that about her. Then she felt the anger rising within, rising from deep within. She looked at Consuela and said, "Well, those people can go to hell!"

Both Margaret and Consuela were surprised at the statement. Margaret Baxter had never expressed such feelings. They looked at each other. Margaret felt more tears roll down her cheeks. She lifted her chin, wiped away the tears and said, "I mean it, Consuela. I'm not living for someone else. I <u>know</u> Joe should not have died. I don't care what anyone else thinks. I'm going to sue."

Consuela was pleased at the strength Margaret was showing. The little mouse had begun to roar. Suddenly, Consuela hoped she had as much strength when she told Fred she was going to sue. She took a deep breath.

"Finally, " Consuela said, "I want to talk to you about the strategy that my dad and I are working on, a strategy that might accomplish what we want quickly."

Consuela explained after the suit was filed, she would conduct a deposition. "Courts order depositions," she explained, "so that the lawyers can examine the people involved in the suit, show some evidence and question those involved. The courts do this because most of the time it saves valuable time in court. Often some charges will be dropped. It is done for efficiency. Usually, the lawyers question only enough to find out certain things but not enough to give away their strategy for the trial."

Margaret nodded her understanding. Consuela then explained the strategy they might try during the deposition. She told Margaret that she believe the doctors hadn't put the facts together. There were many doctors, they were busy and she didn't think they understood what had happened. Boswell should have been putting the facts together but she was convinced that he pretty much had forgotten that Joe was his patient. If he, in fact, hadn't billed for his care that was proof of that. They would reveal their case during the deposition so that the doctors and their lawyers would understand what had happened, to face the truth. Consuela told Margaret that if the strategy worked, the lawyers would convince the doctors and the hospital to settle the case. In fact, she believed the doctors would want to settle the case. Consuela also explained the pitfalls if the strategy didn't work, that at trial the defendants would know what was coming and would have had time to work with their lawyers to carefully craft answers, to mitigate the impact of the facts. Juries tended to trust doctors.

"If they do want to settle, what might they settle for?" asked Margaret.

"I would only be guessing, Margaret. Texas law, unfortunately, limits the amount one can collect in medical malpractice cases. I've calculated that the total of damages and punitive damages in this case will be $3,350,000. I recommend you settle for nothing less."

She saw the shocked look on Margaret's face. "Now Margaret, I remind you that two-thirds of that amount would go to you and one third would go to this law firm. Still, it is a lot of money. If we go to trial, we might win that amount from a jury, or we might win less or nothing at all."

She explained that Margaret would be the one to decide and that she had to balance the cost of going to trial, both actual dollar cost and the huge emotional cost, against the satisfaction of proving in a public trial that the doctors and hospital had acted wrongly, had let Joe die needlessly.

"And," Consuela said, "You need to decide if you want me to try the strategy of revealing most of our case during depositions, believing we will get a settlement. Or, revealing little and going to full trial."

"I will need to think about this, Consuela. I really need to think about this."

"Indeed you do. Why don't I call you after I talk to Dr. Landis?"

"That's fine. And, Consuela, I thank you. I am grateful. I needed to understand why Joe died. Will Marge have a bill ready for the work you've already done?"

"I'm sure she will. Just ask her. And Margaret, stay strong. Pray for guidance."

On Thursday morning Consuela was working at her desk when she heard a commotion in the outer office. She realized it was Cynthia when she heard her yelling, "Tell that girl I've got to see her right now!"

She heard Marge laugh as she opened the door to Consuela's office. There stood Cynthia with a huge grin.

"Girl," boomed Cynthia, "Have I got news for you!"

Consuela laughed and said, "What? Tell me quick before that smile cracks your face. Did Ready to Run tell you he loves you?"

Cynthia laughed and said, "Can't tell you 'til Jim gets here. He's parking the car."

Consuela squealed and jumped from her chair, "You're pregnant!" she shouted and ran to grab Cynthia.

"Yep! We did it!" yelled Cynthia, hugging Consuela and laughing.

The two women stood hugging and jumping up and down. Jim walked in and Consuela grabbed him and yelled, "Congratulations Daddy!"

Jim grinned and hugged Consuela and then put his arms around Cynthia. "How about them apples?" he said, grinning.

"Fantastic!"

"Call Fred. I want to tell him right now," insisted Jim. "I'll tell him how it's done so you guys can get to work. This baby has got to have playmates."

Consuela laughed and went to the phone. When she reached Fred, she said, "Hey, somebody wants to tell you something."

She handed the phone to Jim who said, "Hey, Ace. Guess what. We're going to have a baby!"

Jim and Fred talked a few minutes and then Fred talked to Cynthia and then to Consuela. There was much laughter and excitement. They agreed to have dinner together that night to celebrate.

At dinner, Cynthia refused to drink anything alcoholic. "I'm on the wagon for the duration, folks. I'm taking care of this baby. I'm going to be the best damn pre-natal patient in history!"

They all applauded, Fred clapping the loudest.

"What do your parents think about all this?" asked Fred.

"They're thrilled," answered Cynthia. "Jim's parents are already making plans to come when the baby is born. Mine are elated but I think my mother finds it a little disconcerting. She privately thinks being pregnant is a bit nasty. I think she's mad at God for not providing some other method, some way not to get so huge."

They laughed. They all knew Mrs. Hall was extremely proper and couldn't stand not to look well groomed. She made a point of being dignified and well mannered. Actually, it was surprising that she had ever allowed herself to be pregnant. Certainly, she hadn't bargained on a child like Cynthia, a child who was so unlike her. They clashed often when Cynthia was young, but over time Mrs. Hall had come to accept that Cynthia was Cynthia and there was little she could do about it.

When Cynthia was in her twenties, Mrs. Hall told her one day that she had always loved her but that she had recently realized that she also liked her. Mrs. Hall had found that surprising because Cynthia was loud, too enthusiastic, sometimes used foul language and hung around the race track. She couldn't imagine liking someone like her, but she did.

Cynthia had laughed and given her mother a hug and told her that she loved her, that she also liked her and that was surprising to her too. She allowed as how she usually didn't like snobs, but her mom was an exception.

When Cynthia had married Jim Steelman, both her parents had been thrilled. They adored him. Mr. Hall admired his business sense and the easy, quiet way he moved among the most powerful people in Texas and Washington. Mrs. Hall admired his quiet strength and dignity. She couldn't figure out, however, why he let Cynthia buy race horses. She did know they were deeply in love and happy together. She didn't understand it but she accepted it.

"Listen, Consuela," said Cynthia, "I've got to talk to Maria. There's stuff I want to know about being pregnant and my mother won't be any help. She'll be terrific once the baby is born but Maria loves me and I want to talk to her about being pregnant."

"Cynthia, that will thrill Mother to pieces. Call her tomorrow. Better yet, they're in town. Go see her tomorrow."

"I will."

Friday night Consuela had Fred over for dinner. She had prepared Vitello Tonnato, one of his favorites. She liked serving it because it was prepared in the morning before she went to work and put in the refrigerator and served cold. All she had to fix after work was the Insalata Caprese and she had some great Buffalo mozzarella and fresh basil and tomatoes that actually had taste. They talked about spending their honeymoon in Tuscany.

They talked easily through dinner although Consuela knew she had to warn Fred that she was near filing the lawsuit against the hospital and doctors that he worked with.

They had after dinner coffee in the patio. The sun had set and the cooler air settled over the town.

"Fred, honey," she began, "I feel I have to tell you that I am still working on Joe Baxter's death. I am likely to file suit."

She saw him stiffen and frown. "Great," he said sarcastically.

"This situation is awkward for us, I know. On the one hand I don't want to talk to you about the case because I know you shouldn't be involved. On the other hand, without knowing the facts you'll likely think I'm acting irresponsibly," she said.

"Consuela, you damn lawyers have made it so that if anyone dies, everybody thinks you should sue the doctors."

"Fred, that's not fair. Do you deny that there are some legitimate cases of malpractice?"

"Damn few!"

"What if this is one of those cases?"

"I think the chances of that are from slim to none! You're talking about some excellent doctors and a well run hospital. Consuela, doctors aren't perfect. They do make some mistakes, but mistakes don't necessarily mean malpractice."

"I know that."

"You'd better be damn careful."

"Gosh Fred, I thought I might file just for the fun of it," snapped Consuela.

Fred glared at her for a minute. Then he took a deep breath and said, "I'm sorry. I guess I'm not being fair. I know you'll be sure before you do anything. I just wish you understood this from a doctor's perspective."

"I wish you could understand this from my perspective. I believe that in Joe's case that mistakes, egregious mistakes, were made that lead to his paralysis and death. If that's so, Margaret should be compensated."

"IF, that's so, OK. I'm just saying I find it hard to believe."

"I know that, but without talking to you about the case I can't explain it to you. I'm sure it's better if you can tell the doctors that you don't know anything about the case."

"OK. But you sound like you're definitely going to file. Are you?"

"I'm not positive. But I must tell you that I think so."

"Not going to make me very popular around the hospital," said Fred with a tight smile.

"I know honey. And I'm sorry."

"That's OK. Maybe you'll decide not to file?"

"Maybe," said Consuela, laughing.

"Sweetheart, you're not going to specialize in medical malpractice are you?"

"I can definitely promise you there is no way at all that will happen. No way. My Dad and I decided long ago that we enjoyed general practice rather than a specialized practice. We'd get bored doing the same kind of cases all the time. We actually enjoy exploring new areas."

"Good. I couldn't take it if you specialized in medical malpractice! When are you going to decide whether or not to file?"

"Margaret has to make the final decision. I have an expert looking at the records now. Depends on what he says."

"Great," snapped Fred, his voice rising. "Some two-bit jerkwater doctor will read the file and tell you anything he thinks you want to hear! I know all about the kind of doctor who's willing to testify in malpractice suits!"

Consuela was surprised by his reaction. The sudden outburst showed how sensitive he still was. He was clearly deeply anxious about the case. Perhaps the real storm was yet to come.

Chapter Four

"Fred, I won't even respond to that. Use your head! 'Two bit jerkwater doctors' wouldn't do me any good in the long run. Let's drop it, OK?" Consuela said with some anger in her voice.

"Fine," said Fred, standing. "I'll call you tomorrow."

"Fine," said Consuela.

When Fred left, Consuela quickly cleaned the dining room and went to bed. She found it difficult to sleep.

The next day, Consuela arrived at Cynthia's an hour before the luncheon and bridal shower. She wanted to see if she could help with any last minute work before the party.

Cynthia had everything under control. The house looked beautiful. There were a dozen huge flower arrangements, the Spanish tile floor was sparkling in the sunlight that streamed in from the large windows, the huge dining room table was set for fifteen with sparkling wine goblets, sterling flatware and Cynthia's Limoge china. The centerpiece was a beautiful flower arrangement of purple and white iris and white roses.

"How do you like it?" laughed Cynthia, realizing full well how beautiful it looked.

"Girl, I'm dazzled!"

"Thought you might be. I'm damned pleased myself. Want something to drink?"

"How about some iced tea?"

"Let me get it. Flora and the hired help are running full tilt in the kitchen," said Cynthia heading for the kitchen.

Consuela followed and when she saw Flora she gave her a big hug. Flora had worked for Jim and Cynthia since they had moved into the house. She was about fifty, an outstanding cook and wonderfully efficient. Cynthia simply never had to worry about the house.

"Corazon," said Flora to Consuela. "Que bueno, usted y el doctor! El es muy agradable y muy guapo!"

Consuela laughed and hugged Flora again and said, "Gracias, Flora. Que es el buen odor? Muy rico y sabrosa."

"Es una sopresa. No voy a dicir," said Flora, laughing.

Consuela laughed and followed Cynthia back to the living room. "What are we having?" said Consuela. "Flora won't tell me."

"Me either! But I'm sure we'll love it. I will tell you that Flora made that cold avocado soup you love."

"Fantastic," said Consuela taking a sip of the cold, fresh iced tea. "Hey, little mama, how are you feeling?"

"As a matter of fact, just great! You mother told me to stay in bed for thirty minutes when I wake up and to eat four crackers and an apple. Works like a charm. I haven't been sick yet!"

"Have you told many people that you're pregnant?"

"Girl, I've told everybody who'll listen! I got up at the Junior League meeting and made an announcement and I also made a general announcement in the kitchen at the racetrack."

The doorbell rang and Cynthia went to see who was there. Consuela heard her whoop and say, "Maria, welcome!"

Consuela rushed to the door to hug her mother. Maria looked beautiful and she was smiling radiantly. "Thought I'd see if you needed any last minute help," said Maria.

"I came early for the same reason, but as you can see, the little mother has everything well in hand."

"Cynthia, the house looks so beautiful. I love the flowers."

"Thanks. Do you want something to drink, Maria? Consuela and I are having some iced tea."

"Gracias."

By noon all the guests had arrived. They were served iced tea or Margaritas in the living room and den. Flora had made an assortment of appetizers, which she served on a heavy silver tray.

There was much laughter and light chatter as the women, most of whom had known each other most of their lives, happily greeted each other and exchanged news about their children, bits of gossip, news about their careers or their husbands work. Everyone was solicitous of Margaret Baxter and expressed their sorrow over Joe's death. Although Margaret found it difficult to be the center of so much attention, she bore up well and graciously.

The lunch was superb. The cold avocado soup was followed by "Wedding Chicken", a Southwestern dish made from capon meat in a roux flavored with butter, ground red chili, nutmeg and saffron. Sauteed fresh roasted and peeled green chili, mushrooms, pimento and fresh lemon juice were added at the last minute and the chicken dish was served over diamond shaped pastry squares. It was served with a plate of fresh fruit salad with a poppy-seed dressing. Cynthia had selected one of her favorite California white wines, Conundrum, to serve with the meal.

Coffee and cognac were served after lunch in the living room. Bizcochitos, a crisp, spicy Mexican cookie, and Mexican pralines were placed on silver trays.

Consuela smiled as she saw Mrs. Hall talking to her mother. Mrs. Hall had certainly not approved of Bill Travis marrying Maria, but over the years, as Consuela and Cynthia had become such close friends and it became evident that Maria was simply not concerned about whether Mrs. Hall liked her or not, Mrs. Hall had come to admire Maria, even to like her.

When it came time to open the gifts, Consuela was overwhelmed. Each gift was so carefully chosen and reflected not only Consuela's taste but something about the woman who had given the gift. Consuela knew she would treasure each gift and think about her friends whenever she saw them.

Cynthia Hall Steelman knew how to do something elegant and comfortable at the same time.

Consuela wished Fred could have seen how beautiful the house looked. She was anxious to show him the gifts. God, she thought, let Fred get over being mad.

Consuela was in her office when Dr. Landis called. Marge put the call through and Consuela said, "Hi Dr. Landis. Good of you to call."

"Hello Miss Travis. I've had an interesting weekend reading Joe Baxter's file. I want to tell you what I've found and give you some advice. OK?"

"Yes, I appreciate your efforts."

Dr. Landis told her he felt the emergency surgery on Joe had been well handled and had, without doubt, saved his life. He felt the gastronomy was questionable but within standard practice.

"I want you to understand, Miss Travis," he continued, "the initial X-ray that pictured only the first five cervical vertebrae is not unusual. Large, muscular men often pose a problem in cervical X-rays because the muscle mass makes it difficult to show the first seven vertebrae. Not unusual at all."

He then said, "However, since Joe Baxter had a cut on his forehead and <u>particularly</u> since he complained of numbness and had a weak bilateral hand grasp, better X-rays should have been made or a CAT scan done. By the way, doing an X-ray initially, instead of a CAT scan, is proper procedure because the X-ray is fast and easy and can be done in the operating room. In my judgement, given the nature of Baxter's symptoms of a cervical spine injury, the failure to get an X-ray that showed the first seven vertebrae within a short time post-operatively was a violation of good, standard medical practice."

Consuela was writing notes rapidly and concentrating on what Dr. Landis was saying but she did manage to nod her head and smile slightly. She had been right.

Dr. Landis continued, "Absent the proper X-ray, at a minimum Joe Baxter should have had a hard collar placed around his neck until a proper X-ray had been made so that spinal chord injury could be ruled out. Failure to do so was a violation of good, standard medical practice."

Dr. Landis then pointed out that once the Vinke brace had been placed on Joe, the doctors failed to pay attention to the G-tube incision which was partially obscured by the brace.

"Miss Travis, when the Vinke brace was placed and they started him on steroids without paying attention to the gastronomy tube incision, the most serious breach of standard practice ensued. The steroids clearly inhibited the healing of the incision and it quickly became infected. The body does not fight infection well when massive steroids are used. The gastronomy incision is an area of plentiful Candida. The systemic candidiasis bloomed there, they didn't see it because of the Vinke brace, and the steroids turned the infection into systemic infection, and thus he died. This is a shocking breach of standard medical practice."

Consuela felt vindicated. She had figured it out! She and Dr. Landis discussed several other things. He had no explanation for the paucity of notes by Dr. Boswell. He certainly found it odd that he was listed as the Admitting Doctor but had written almost no notes. Dr. Landis said he couldn't say whether it was malpractice because he didn't know what explanation there might be.

Then Consuela said she had just discovered that Dr. Boswell had sent no bills to the Baxters. Dr. Landis said that really did seem to indicate that he had forgotten Joe Baxter was his patient and had never informed his office that Baxter was a patient.

Dr. Landis did say the fact that Boswell hadn't written the discharge note until long after Baxter's death really did bother him. That was a clear violation of the accrediting standards of the American Hospital Association. It was not, however, a sign of malpractice since the patient was already dead.

Chapter Four

It was clear that Doctors Boswell and Patterson had failed to consider the effect of steroids administered by Doctors Roberts and Morales and equally clear that Roberts and Morales had failed to consider the effect of steroids on the G-tube incision.

"Miss Travis, this is a case of the patient falling through the cracks. Too many doctors, each of them taking a narrow view of what they were doing and no one looking at the whole patient. Dr. Boswell should have been looking at the whole patient and there is nothing to show he did. He should be held accountable. It is also clear that the doctors should have paid attention to the nurses. Ofelia Ortiz's notes clearly track what was happening. I'll bet they never read her notes. Most doctors don't read the nurse's reports. I checked and found that Memorial Hospital is about to computerize their records. It's about time. Dr. Morales' handwriting is illegible, even for a doctor."

Dr. Landis said he believed Joe would have had only limited use of his left leg and foot had he survived, but clearly, he should have survived.

Finally, Dr. Landis said, "Miss Travis, you have a clear and convincing case of medical malpractice. I will testify for you if you go to trial."

Consuela said, "Dr. Landis I can't tell you how grateful I am for your attention to this case, for your quick attention. I feel confident now. As you know, my burden of proof at trial would be a preponderance of the evidence. I am thrilled that you believe we surpass that standard to a clear and convincing case. You and I came to the same conclusions but I am not a doctor so I couldn't be sure I was right. I was prepared to drop this case if you said I didn't have a case. My father and I followed your advice several years ago and didn't file a malpractice case. Thank you! I'll have Marge send you a check today. Don't write your report until I ask you. I'm hoping to settle the case before the 90 day deadline. I'll let you know what happens and if we'll need you at trial."

Later that day, Consuela talked to her father and to Margaret. They all agreed to file the medical malpractice lawsuit.

Fred took Consuela out to dinner that night and their conversation was careful. He sensed that she was tense and he thought he knew why. During dinner, Consuela steered the conversation toward topics like Cynthia's luncheon, the gifts, their new house plans. Fred was happy to talk about these things, not wanting to talk about a malpractice suit in a restaurant.

As soon as they walked in the door of Consuela's house, Fred said, "OK, Consuela. Let's have it. You're as nervous as a cat."

"We've got to talk. Let me fix some Drambuie and coffee."

"Fine. I'll be in the patio."

When she came out, Fred had taken off his coat and removed his tie. He was stretched out in a chair, his long legs reaching far under the table. His eyes were closed and Consuela realized how tired he was. She knew he had been in surgery most of the day. He sure wasn't going to be in a very good mood to hear about a medical malpractice suit, she thought.

He opened his eyes as she put the tray on the table and sat down. They both drank some Drambuie and looked at each other.

"Let's have it, " he said.

"I'm going to file the suit," she said quietly.

"Shit!"

"Fred, I'm sorry. I know you wish I weren't involved in this, but I am. I feel it is what I have to do."

"Great. Just great. And great timing too. I just got notification that my malpractice insurance is going up to $100,000 next year. And I've never been sued!"

"I'm sorry."

"I'll just bet you are."

"Fred, be fair."

"Let me tell you about fair. Every doctor I know works like a dog. All of us are hitting it twelve, fourteen hours a day. I'm always tired, always worried about some patient, some operation, something. Honest to God, Consuela, I do the best I can and it pisses me off that someday something will go wrong and I'll get sued. And I'll get sued whether I deserve it or not."

Consuela didn't answer. There was little she could say. She knew that some doctors had been sued unfairly. Some lawyers were unethical. She thought she understood Fred's resentment.

"I wish to God more lawyers got sued for malpractice!" Fred said angrily.

"I know there are some who richly deserve it. Lawyers do as bad a job as doctors policing themselves."

"Do you really have to do this?"

"Yes."

"Who are you going to name in the suit?"

"Boswell, Patterson, Roberts, Morales, Webster and the hospital."

"Good God, Consuela. Have you lost your mind? You're filing suit on an excellent group of doctors. I know these guys. They work hard and are damned skilled. You can't be serious!" Fred shouted.

"I am," said Consuela, struggling to keep calm. "I believe they committed malpractice in treating Joe Baxter. I believe their malpractice lead to his death. I'm convinced of it and convinced I can prove it in court."

"They may have made mistakes. No doctor is perfect. We're just human. We get tired, distracted, exhausted. You're saying they killed him."

"Fred, I'm saying they committed malpractice that lead to his death. I am not saying they intended him harm. They didn't mean to kill him. But they did."

"How, for God's sake?"

"Do you really want me to tell you?"

"No. Never mind. Why do you go after doctors like a bloodsucker?"

"Fred, I resent that!" said Consuela, her voice rising. "How dare you call me a bloodsucker!"

"Because malpractice lawyers are bloodsuckers, that's why!"

Consuela gritted her teeth, her anger mounting. "I think you better leave. I will not sit here and let you call me names."

"I'll be glad to leave," said Fred standing abruptly and grabbing his jacket. He stood there for a moment, his jaw clenched. He was waiting, Consuela thought, for her to say she wouldn't file the suit. She just looked at him.

He took a deep breath and said, "Maybe we better reconsider the marriage while we're at it."

"Fine. If you think you're marrying some little girl who has to do what you want and only what you want, think again buddy!"

Her heart was pounding. She knew they were both angry and might regret what they were saying, but she realized this was a side of Fred she'd never seen. If he refused to trust her legal judgement and if he intended to spend their married life telling her what she could and couldn't do, she needed to find that out now.

Fred started to say something, then shut his mouth, turned and walked away.

Consuela was shaking in anger and fear when he left. She was furious with him. She was afraid that their relationship might be over.

She sat in the patio chair, crying, for more than an hour. She prayed to God for understanding and comfort. She hoped Fred would come back and apologize. He didn't.

She awoke the following morning with a pounding headache. She felt empty and alone as her mind flooded with memories of the night before.

She was brushing her teeth when she heard the doorbell ring. She rinsed her mouth and walked to the door, hoping, praying it was Fred. She had always known she loved him, but during a night, thinking she might have lost him, she realized how deeply she loved him, how desperately she wanted to spend the rest of her life with him. Their relationship had never really been tested. Now that it had been, she was in a turmoil of mixed emotions: fury at him for not trusting her, desperately in love with him, fear that she had lost him, and an enduring unwillingness to drop the suit.

She opened the door and saw him standing there, the early morning sun glinting off his soft brown hair. They looked at each other for a moment, neither one able to speak.

He opened his arms and with a sharp cry she fell into them. He wrapped her in his strong arms and squeezed. When she looked up she saw he had tears in his eyes.

"God, I love you," he said gently.

"Oh Fred, I need you so much. I love you. I realized last night how much."

"Me too," said Fred as he held her back from his body so he could see her face. "Consuela, I acted like a child. I'm ashamed of myself and I apologize."

"Let me apologize too for saying ugly things. Fred, can't we work this out?"

"Only if you fix me breakfast," he said, laughing.

Consuela beamed as she lead him into the kitchen. They kissed each other for several long minutes as they stood by the stove, both wanting to reassure themselves that everything was alright again.

As they ate breakfast, they talked. Neither held anything back, both saying how miserable they had been all night, both saying the fight was probably a good thing since it showed them how much they loved each other.

"But Fred, " said Consuela, "You do understand I am going ahead with this case?"

"Yes, of course. I still don't like it but I realized I was not trusting you. Consuela, I've known you for so many years and I <u>know</u> your judgement is excellent. If you think you should file, you should. I guess I was worried about the flack I will have to take at the hospital. That was selfish."

"But damned understandable!" said Consuela, reaching for his hand. "I am truly sorry that you will be made uncomfortable by this."

Consuela stopped, trying to grasp a thought that had been percolating in her unconscious mind all night. It came like a flash and she immediately knew it was right. "Fred, I thought about this most of the night. I am going ahead with Margaret's case, but I have decided I will never again get involved in a medical malpractice suit. It is simply unfair to you and I won't do it again."

Fred smiled. He knew how difficult it was for her to say that. He loved her for her willingness to exclude medical malpractice from her law practice. "Consuela," he said, "I am not asking you to do that."

She laughed and said, "Honey, I know you're not. If you'd asked I probably would have refused. But if I'm going to marry a doctor it seems prudent not to do medical malpractice cases. I'm completely comfortable with the decision. Are you?"

"Yes. But I want you to know that whether or not you do malpractice cases, I want to marry you. Understand?"

"Thank you. But this is the last one. I love you."

They could both feel the tension drain away and the solid sense of their love for each other return.

They took their coffee outside to the patio and looked at the early morning sunshine giving color and depth to the mountain. A mockingbird was singing in a tree nearby, his melody soaring into the still morning.

"You know what? The Celts were right," Consuela said. "I do see God in the faces of people, in all his creation like that wonderful mountain, the singing of that bird. I see him in you."

Consuela called Margaret when she got to the office and asked if she could come in that afternoon. Margaret said she would be there at two.

Consuela spent the morning working with her father getting all the papers ready to file. Bill had only a few suggestions to make as he read the draft Consuela had written and by noon Marge Kern had the documents ready.

Consuela and Bill decided to have lunch in the small café in the building and as they sat eating green enchiladas, made with green chiles and tomatillas, Bill asked if she had told Fred she was going to file the suit.

"Yep, last night. He was mad as hell but by this morning he was alright. But, Daddy, I told him this morning that I wouldn't take another medical malpractice case."

"Did he ask you to promise him that?"

"Nope. Strictly my idea."

"Smart man," said Bill.

"Is it OK with you if this is my last medical malpractice case?"

"Sugar, of course. I know better than to try to tell you what kind of law to practice!"

"Chip off the old block, huh?"

"You bet!"

"Any second thoughts about filing this case?"

"No. I promised Margaret and I want to see it through. I feel like I have to. Understand?"

"Yes."

That afternoon Consuela went over the case carefully with Margaret. She outlined the procedures they would face and the possibly very long timetable they might well have to endure. She told Margaret she still had hope they might be able to settle the case after the first couple of depositions because she believed the doctors had never put all the facts together. But, she made clear, they still might be unwilling to settle for the very large amount that Consuela thought Margaret deserved. If they had to go to court, Margaret would face an emotional toll and have to endure ugly remarks some people were sure to make. They could loose at trial and Margaret would still have to pay Consuela's expenses. She wanted to make sure Margaret understood what they were facing.

"Do you still want to go ahead?"

"Yes. Consuela, I've thought about this a lot. I drove to Marfa and talked to Joe's parents and mine. We all agree that the suit should go forward. And, by the way, Joe's dad is an accountant. He studied the Texas law and did some figuring and agreed that the three million plus dollar figure is just about right. So, do it."

"OK, I'll get Marge to bring the papers in for you to sign, including the contract with me. I want you to read the contract carefully before you sign it and I'll explain anything you don't understand. OK?"

"Fine."

Chapter Four

After Margaret read and signed the papers, she said, "There is one other thing I want to talk to you about. I want your advice."

"Sure. What is it?"

"I'm thinking about selling the farm. I've had to face the fact that I'm just not cut-out to run a farm all by myself. I haven't wanted to sell because somehow it is like selling a part of Joe."

"I can understand that, but I can also understand that trying to run the farm alone is no picnic either. Do you have a buyer?"

"Yes. Mr. Hamilton, who has the farm next to ours and who has been helping me, has made an offer."

"Is the offer reasonable?"

Margaret smiled and said, "You'll be proud of me. I've talked to three real estate agents and I had an appraiser come out and do an official appraisal. Mr. Hamilton's offer is very reasonable."

Consuela was astonished. The old Margaret would never have had the gumption to do all that. "Good for you!" said Consuela.

Margaret grinned and nodded her head.

"Are you going to move back to Marfa when you sell?"

"I don't think so. I just know that my parents, and Joe's too, will be so concerned about me being alone that they would smother me. I'm going to stay here, I think."

Consuela nodded her head and said, "That's probably smart. You've got lots of friends here, people who care about you."

"I know. It has taken me a long time to come to grips with my life without Joe. I'm sure not fully adjusted to the idea, there are still lots of bad days. But I am stronger. Funny thing is, Joe had been talking to me about being more independent. Maybe I'm doing some of this for him," said Margaret, tears starting to well up in her eyes.

Consuela nodded her head.

Margaret look at Consuela and said, "You know the last thing Joe said to me? He'd been kind of in and out of consciousness for a few days. Sometimes when he was conscious, he was downright psychotic...but this time I could tell from his eyes that he was OK. He looked at me and said, 'Honey, it's OK for you to cut your hair.' Then he closed his eyes, a smile on his face. That's the last thing he said." Tears began to stream down her face.

"How strange," said Consuela.

"I thought so too, but I realized later what he was really saying. He'd been talking to me about being more assertive, more independent. I tried, but it was really difficult for me. You know how I always was, it was just easier for me to agree with everyone. In any case, a few days before the wreck, I told Joe I thought I would get my hair cut. He was furious, just hated the idea and told me so, told me he loved my long hair. I quickly said I wouldn't get it cut. I think he felt guilty. He'd been telling me to be independent and assertive and then when I wanted to get my hair cut, he told me not to. What he said to me in the hospital was his way of telling me to be independent. I'm sure of it."

"I'll be damned," said Consuela. "I'll bet you're right."

"So, I'm learning to do it. I am going to sell the farm. I'll talk to Mr. Hamilton tonight. Will you do the legal work for me? I can pay you for that out of the proceeds from the sale, " said Margaret, laughing.

"Certainly. Send me a copy of your deed and I'll get to work on it. Marge has a form that you can fill out with her. That should give me all the information I need."

Consuela walked to the outer office with Margaret and told Marge that Margaret was going to sell the farm and the firm would handle the sale. She said, "Please give Margaret the necessary forms and tell her what she needs to bring you."

Consuela hugged Margaret and told her to stay in touch. When she went back into her office, Consuela spent a few minutes thinking about all Margaret had been through and how it seemed to be making her stronger instead of destroying her. Funny, thought Consuela, how things sometimes work out.

Fred and Consuela spent most of the weekend watching the construction of their house. The foundation, the framing, the electrical and plumbing work had been completed and they watched the baked adobe walls begin to rise, watched the house begin to take shape. They were pleased with the work their builder, Jose Solis, had taken to save almost all the trees. A beautiful pecan tree stood proudly in the patio with the walls rising around it.

Jim and Cynthia brought them a picnic lunch on Saturday and the four of them sat under a large, old pecan tree, staying cool while they ate.

Cynthia's pregnancy was beginning to show, much to her delight. She emphasized the slight thickening around her waist by wearing an oversized maternity T-shirt. Jim was especially solicitous and always made sure Cynthia was comfortable. They had brought fold-up chairs so Cynthia could sit comfortably.

After lunch, while Jim and Fred talked to Jose, Consuela and Cynthia stayed under the tree chatting about the baby and the new house.

Chapter Four

Consuela told Cynthia about the fight she had with Fred. Cynthia was relieved that the issue had been resolved and agreed with Consuela that not taking any more medical malpractice cases was a good idea.

On Sunday they had prayed at the early service at St. Clement's Episcopal Church that God would help them through the lawsuit and the building of their house . That afternoon they were walking around when the workers arrived. They had agreed to pay the workers time and a half for working Sunday afternoons, not only because they were in a hurry to get the house done, but because during the week they were so busy they couldn't get to the site and they wanted to watch their house being built, wanted to feel part of the construction. They had also paid Jose Solis to hire extra workers during the week.

Solis agreed to let them lay the adobe for part of one wall, after some expert instruction from one of the workers. Under close supervision, they completed the line of adobe. The supervisor, having had to make them re-do only a few pieces, was pleased with their work. He laughed and said he might be willing to take them on as apprentices.

That night they took a long, soaking bath to get off all the dust and to soak the kinks out of their backs from the lifting and leaning they had done laying the line of adobe.

Fred called and had a pizza delivered and they snuggled in front of the TV. Their wedding was now only a month away and the house should be finished before then.

They discussed buying some new furniture to supplement what they already owned and had a mock fight about an old, tattered chair Fred had had since he was in medical school. He insisted he wanted to keep it and Consuela finally said OK as long as it stayed in his study and no one ever saw it.

They both agreed that the new furniture should be bought in Juarez because they loved the hand carved pieces many of their friends had and which decorated much of Bill and Maria's house. They dreaded the trip to Juarez which had, during the past decade, become an ordeal going through immigration and customs inspections, but they agreed it would be worth it.

They went to bed early. They slept half-entwined, happy to be together and happy they had overcome the pain of the fight about the malpractice suit. The weekend had been a time of closeness and excitement about their new home.

Chapter Five
The Deposition

During the next two weeks Fred did share with Consuela the consternation at the hospital about the malpractice lawsuit. He had been the recipient of several ugly cracks about his fiancee but when it became clear that Fred knew nothing about the suit and that he was not going to respond to remarks about Consuela except to look coldly at the person talking, he stopped hearing anything. Fred was highly skilled and admired, and although the doctors were uniformly furious at Consuela, they stopped holding Fred responsible. The case was not discussed in his presence.

Consuela received a call from Walt Urban, the attorney who had been hired to represent the hospital. After a few pointed remarks about malpractice lawsuits in general, Urban said, "Miss Travis, I just called to tell you that I am considering filing an abuse of process case against you."

"That's your privilege, Mr. Urban. Go right ahead," said Consuela, keeping her anger under control. Consuela knew the case wasn't frivolous and that Urban didn't have a prayer of winning an abuse of process case. What made her furious was the sleazy attempt to intimidate her.

"If you think I'm kidding, think again Miss Travis."

"Mr. Urban, I wouldn't dream that you're kidding!" said Consuela in mock horror. "Be my guest."

"I just might do that."

"Fine. Nice to talk to you counselor," said Consuela as she hung up the phone.

Consuela called her father at the ranch. "Hey Pop," she said when he answered the phone. "Walt Urban just called and threatened to file an abuse of process case against me."

"That old fraud!" said Bill, laughing. "What did you say to him?"

"I told him to be my guest."

"Good for you. That's the last you'll hear about that. I guarantee you. Have the depositions been scheduled yet?"

"Not yet. I suggested the first week in November. That would give them a few weeks to prepare but not too much time and would be after the wedding and honeymoon. And the first week in November would be before the 90 day requirement to file the outside expert's report for each defendant. If they buy the date for the depositions, we won't have to give them Dr Landis' report."

"Good. I think Urban is arrogant enough to want to do it early to show we're incompetent. Only his client, Francisco Catron, the hospital administrator, has easy access to the full record and he isn't a doctor. The others would have to pay to have the whole record copied. I'll bet that Walt Urban hasn't read the whole record, much less analyzed it, and I'll also bet the others haven't paid to have the whole record copied. They will have just looked at their clients part of the record. Let's keep our fingers crossed. Stay in touch, baby girl."

"I will, Dad. Give my love to Mom."

When Consuela hung up, Marge came into her office with a stack of papers. "Here are the papers for Margaret's closing on the sale of the farm. We got the papers back from the title company. Everything's ready to go."

"Great! Marge, what would I do without you?"

"Go broke, probably," answered Marge, laughing.

The closing was held that afternoon. Both Frank Hamilton and his wife Sarah were seated across the table from Margaret. When the final papers were signed, Frank turned to Sarah and said, "Let's give them the flowers now."

Sarah reached into a large bag she had carried in and took out two huge bouquets of yellow roses and handed them to Margaret and Consuela. "Pleasure doing business with the Yellow Roses of Texas" she said.

After the Hamilton's left, Margaret and Consuela sat and talked. Margaret said, "Consuela, I wanted you to know that I have hired an accountant and he's giving me some investment advice. I have to be careful with the money I got today. I intend to put the maximum amount into an IRA and then buy some triple exempt municipal bonds. What do you think?"

"Sounds fine to me. That stuff really isn't my strong suit, however. Who's the accountant?"

"Marvin Chapman."

"Well, you've gotten a top ranked accountant. He's good. How did you happen to pick him?"

Chapter Five

Margaret laughed and said, "He's an Aggie. I remembered him from all those Aggie parties. He's a nice man."

Consuela laughed and said, "Well, I'll forgive him for going to A&M and he is a nice man."

"I've rented a house way up on Wheeling Street, just before it intersects with Scenic Drive. I looked at a few places over on this side of the mountain, but I wanted to be able to see the lower valley, down toward San Elizario, if I could. This house has a great view of the lower valley and the river. It is quiet and has plenty of room. And, I'm relieved to say, it is not too expensive."

"Good for you. When are you moving?"

"On Monday. I've left my new telephone number with Marge and I've written it on this card for you," she said, handing the card to Consuela.

"Can I do anything to help?"

"Thanks, but I can handle it. My parents are coming this weekend to help. They're not too thrilled about my moving to the house. They thought I ought to move back to Marfa, but they've accepted it and are being really helpful."

"Well, give them my love."

"I will."

"Will you be able to take that big dog with you?"

Margaret laughed and said, "Of course! Barton made finding a place to live a little difficult, but I wouldn't consider not having him. That's one of the best things about the house. It has a fenced yard and the owners live next door and love dogs. Their dog died this summer and they're thrilled to have Barton."

"How great!"

"Isn't it! And I am only a few blocks away from St. Alban's Episcopal Church. You know the one on Elm Street?"

"Sure."

"I went by there the day I rented the house to thank God for helping me find it. I was sitting in the church when the rector came in to do something, saw me and came over to ask if he could help me. We talked awhile. I really liked him and I'm going to transfer my membership there."

"Thanks be to God," said Consuela. She realized that Margaret was smiling fully, nothing held back. That was the first time she had seen Margaret really smile since Joe had died.

"What about your own house when you and Fred move into the new one?" asked Margaret.

"Mom and Dad have decided to sell it. They were happy to let me live there because they didn't have to worry about anything, but they just don't want to bother renting. They'll put it on the market after our wedding. Interested?"

"No. I'm comfortable with what I'm doing," said Margaret and Consuela saw that same full smile.

Walt Urban, the hospital's attorney, called Consuela the next day. When Marge told her who was on the line, Consuela couldn't believe it. What did he want now, she wondered, was he going to threaten her again?

"Hello, Mr. Urban," she said, trying to sound pleasant.

"Miss Travis, I'm calling on behalf of all the defendants. We certainly do not want to wait six weeks for the depositions! We all want to get rid of this nuisance and insist that we have depositions in two weeks."

Consuela was shocked. Defense attorneys usually tried to postpone, not hurry up, depositions. She was sure they had deliberately picked a date just before her wedding. But she also realized that the attorney's certainly had not had time to study Joe Baxter's extensive medical record, they hadn't gotten her expert testimony which was required within 90 days of filing, that they were just taking the word of their clients that they had done nothing wrong. She was convinced that none of them had put the facts together. This could work in her favor, she thought, because they wouldn't know enough to adequately advise their clients.

"Let me look at my calendar, Mr. Urban. What dates do you have in mind?"

"The fifteenth and sixteenth."

"How about the fourteenth and fifteenth instead?" said Consuela.

"Uhh...the fourteenth and fifteenth? You could be ready then?" he asked with a slight choking sound.

"I could be ready anytime, Mr. Urban."

"OK Consuela, we'll call your bluff! I'll see you on the fourteenth. At your office?"

"Yes. I'll hire a court reporter and be ready to go. Let's start at four in the afternoon so the doctors who want to attend will be able to. I'll send

CHAPTER FIVE

you a list of whom I will depose on each day. Those people will, of course, have to attend on their assigned day."

"Fine."

Consuela hung up and called her father. She recounted the conversation. "Those bastards," he said. "They know when your wedding is and thought they'd put the fear in you. Can you really be ready on the fourteenth? When are you moving in your house? What can I do to help?"

"It's going to be tough but I can do it. We're moving this weekend. You and Mom can certainly help with that. We've got the movers lined up. It just means I won't get to futz around the house much until after the honeymoon. And if you could spend the thirteenth with me going over the material for the deposition and helping me word some questions, that would be great."

"Of course. That Walt Urban makes me really mad. We'll show him not to mess around with you. I agree that they couldn't have really studied the case. Hope he's so arrogant that they don't before the depositions and you'll hit them between the eyes."

"Dad, there is one good thing about all this. Maybe I can put all this to rest at the depositions and have my marriage ceremony and honeymoon without having to worry about all this."

"From your mouth to God's ear. But, honey, Urban is a stubborn guy. His practice is limited to defending people in malpractice cases. He knows we're general practice lawyers and that he has lots more experience in this area than we do. It may well be that they won't offer to settle."

"You're right. But I think he suffers from thinking he knows more than anyone about medical malpractice and doesn't do his homework. We had to do lots of homework but we discovered the truth. Well, let's get ready to play our hand and see what they've got."

Early Saturday morning the movers arrived at Fred's apartment and Consuela's house. They supervised the packing and then met later at the new house. Maria and Bill and the Steelman's were there to help. Cynthia supervised the placement of the furniture and paintings in the living room, Consuela supervised the master bedroom and bathroom, Maria took care of the kitchen, breakfast room and dining room, Fred supervised the placement of the outdoor furniture in the patio and in the large study which he was to share with Consuela, and Jim oversaw the extra bedrooms and bathrooms. By six o'clock they were done.

Fred poured iced tea for Cynthia and made Margaritas for everyone else. They all collapsed in chairs under the overhang in the patio. Maria raised her glass and said, "Amor y pesetas y tiempo para gustarlo!"

They cheered and took a drink, Cynthia raised her glass and said, "Y muchos muchachos! My kid needs playmates!" Laughter filled the patio as they raised their glasses.

Jim raised his glass and said, "The Celtic Blessing, if you please." They joined him and said, "Life is short and we do not have much time to gladden the hearts of those who travel with us, so be quick to love and make haste to be kind!" They drank to the toast.

Fred then said, "OK, the Irish toast!" They all laughed and raised their glasses and said, "May the roof over our heads never fall in and the friends below never fall out!" They cheered and drank.

Cynthia announced, "Folks, I've been sitting here looking out at that pool in the middle of the patio and I can't stand it another minute. We swim!"

Consuela managed to find swimsuits for Maria and herself but Cynthia was now too large to fit into one, so she ordered Jim, Fred and her father to go relax in the large Jacuzzi in the master bathroom. When they left, Cynthia stripped and dove in, surfacing at the other end of the pool. She shouted, "Girls, this is heaven. Get in!"

After swimming for awhile the women got out and dressed. Bill was the first to return from the Jacuzzi and he announced to Maria, "Sweetheart. You gotta try that! I think we need one for the ranch."

On Monday Consuela and Bill talked about the depositions that were scheduled the next day. They concentrated on Randy Patterson, the surgical resident who assisted Sam Boswell perform the surgery, including the gastrostomy, and on Paul Morales who was the orthopedic surgeon who assisted Dan Roberts and whose handwriting was virtually illegible. They intended to fully explore the issues with these two and then move the next day to Simon Webster, the radiologist, Francisco Catron, the hospital administrator, Dan Roberts, the orthopedic surgeon, and, finally, to Sam Boswell, who was listed as the admitting doctor and thus the doctor in charge.

After a full day of work with her father, Consuela felt ready.

That night she and Fred had dinner at home, a simple chicken salad. They ate in the breakfast room. Fred knew the depositions started the next day and he wanted to help Consuela by having a peaceful night, an evening when they could just enjoy their new home.

"You know what I really like about this room?" he asked.

Consuela looked around the room and smiled. "That small picture over there that was taken in the Winner's Circle the day Ready to Run won the sweepstakes?"

Fred laughed and said, "You got it! Cynthia stuck it up there on Saturday as a joke. I think we should keep it up. What do you think?"

"Absolutely! We all won a bunch of money and it was fun! What's your favorite thing in the living room?"

Fred thought a minute and said, "The furniture we had made in Juarez. I love the look and feel of the fabric and the handsome carving on the couches and coffee table."

"Me too, but I must say my favorite thing is the painting on the left wall, that one by Peter Hurd that Cynthia made me buy when I graduated from college. I didn't have the money, but the art dealer in Old Mesilla let me pay it out on time. That wall is perfect for it."

"I'll tell you the art work I have grown to really love, that pen and ink portrait of your dad that Tom Lea did. There's one by Tom Lea in the doctor's lounge, a portrait of Dr. Bob Homan. I love that we've put the portrait of your dad in the study."

"Me too," said Consuela, nodding in agreement.

They cleaned the dishes, soaked in the Jacuzzi and went to bed.

Consuela looked around the room and said, "May I have your attention. The time to begin the depositions has arrived. Many of you know Linda Martinez, the court reporter. She is here to keep a record of these proceedings. Let me begin by noting that the court issued and served the notice of depositions to be held on November third and fourth. Mr. Urban called and said he represented all the parties in this case and requested a re-schedule of the depositions to this time. I agreed and the court was notified of the change."

Consuela saw a frown cross Judy Martin's face. She apparently wasn't pleased with Walt Urban's effort.

Consuela continued, "Let us go around the table and state our names so that Miss Martinez can create a record. I am Consuela Travis. I represent Margaret Baxter, the widow of Joe Baxter."

"Chris Sharp, representing Dr. Randolph Patterson."

"Dr. Randy Patterson."

"Judy Martin, representing Dr. Paul Morales."

"Dr. Paul Morales."

"Walter Urban, I represent Dr. Sam Boswell, Dr. Simon Webster and Francisco Catron."

"Francisco Catron, the head administrator of Memorial Hospital."

"Dr. Simon Webster."

"Dr. Sam Boswell."

"Jorge Lopez, representing Dr. Don Roberts."

"Dr. Don Roberts."

Consuela smiled and said, "Thank you. I will now hand each of you sections of Joe Baxter's medical records about which I will be a asking questions. I have numbered the pages so you can find the right page quickly. "

The attorney's were surprised Normally, the records were handed out only as the attorney conducting the deposition raised questions about some entry and then only that entry was handed to the person being questioned and to their attorney. Consuela had noticed that only Walt Urban, who represented Francisco Catron, the hospital administrator, had a huge folder, containing, she was sure, the full record. Just as she suspected, the other lawyers had only small folders, containing, she was sure, only their client's part of the record.

Consuela saw Walt Urban grinning at some of the other attorneys and raising his eyebrows. It was clear Urban didn't think Consuela knew what the hell she was doing. Consuela was almost certain that they had talked to their clients but hadn't really studied the record.

"Now Dr. Patterson, if you'll come sit here in this chair near the court reporter, we can get started."

Randy Patterson shrugged and moved to the chair. Linda Martinez, the court reporter, turned to him and said, "Please state your name and raise your right hand and repeat after me, 'I swear to tell the truth, the whole truth and nothing but the truth, so help me God.' " He did as directed.

Consuela turned to Patterson and said, "Dr. Patterson, where did you get your medical degree?"

"From the Baylor College of Medicine in Houston."

"Where did you do your internship?"

"At Memorial Hospital."

"Here in El Paso?"

"Yes."

"What is your position now?"

Chapter Five

"I am a resident."
"You are not yet an attending?"
"That is correct."
"You participated in the initial surgery on Joe Baxter?"
"Yes."
"With whom were you working?"
"Dr. Boswell."
"Did he do the G-tube?"
"No."
"Did you?"
"Yes."
"Was it your idea to do that procedure?"

Randy Patterson shifted slightly in his seat. He glanced briefly at Dr. Boswell , who maintained a calm look on his face. Randy said, "Not exactly."

"Did someone suggest it?"
"Yes."
"Who?"
"Dr. Boswell."
"Do you know why?"
" Because Mr. Baxter might not be able to eat normally for a few days. To keep his nutrition up."
"Was it part of your duties to check on Joe Baxter while he was in the hospital?"
"Yes."
"Did you check on his leg in the cast?"
"No. That was the orthopedic doctors job. I did read his charts to see how it was coming."
"Was it important for you to know what the orthopods were doing?"
"Of course."
"Why was it important?"
"Because it could impact on the treatment I was administering."
"Did you read Dr. Don Robert's Doctors Progress Report?"
"Yes."
"Every day?"
"I believe so. Every day I was on duty."
"What about the Doctors Progress Report of Dr Paul Morales?"
"Yes."

"I'm going to hand you some of Dr. Morales' reports. Read the first one out loud, please."

A look of distress came across Randy Patterson's face. He took the report and opened it to the first page. He squinted at the report. He looked at Dr. Morales. He tried to read the report. "I think it says that the leg was...something...that the cast must...something....I'm sorry. I can't read it."

"That's OK. Let's try the report on page five."

Randy Patterson turned to page five and stared at the entry. "I see he prescribed morphine sulfate." He looked at Consuela and said, "That's for pain."

Consuela nodded and smiled. "Read the rest of the entry."

Randy stared at the writing. "Something about...I think it says 'traction'...then 'the cast'..then...I'm sorry. I can't quite make it out."

The lawyers began to be uneasy. They began to shuffle through the large stack of documents Consuela had given them at the beginning of the hearing. They found the page numbers Consuela had asked Randy Patterson about. She saw all but Judy Martin looking puzzled and surprised. Judy had clearly tried to read her client's handwriting and knew it was illegible. Consuela was almost certain that the others hadn't looked at it. Walt Urban's move to make the depositions early had left them little time.

Walt Urban suddenly said, "I object!"

Consuela looked at him and said, "Mr. Urban, you know objections can't be raised in a deposition. But, I'll humor you. On what basis do you object?"

"Umm..what does this have to do with malpractice?"

"I believe you'll see during the day today."

Consuela looked at Linda Martinez and said "Miss Martinez, did you get all that?"

Linda Martinez, the court reporter, said, "Yes."

"OK," said Consuela. "Now what does the rest of the entry say?"

"I'm sorry. I can't read but a few words."

"Now Dr. Patterson, when you can't read a doctor's entry, you then read the Nurses Progress Report, right?"

"Uh..not usually."

"Are you saying you sometimes read the Nurses Progress Report?"

"I guess."

"OK. Do you know Orelia Ortiz?"

"Yes."
"Who is she?"
"She works in intensive care."
"Did she help care for Joe Baxter?"
"Yes."
"Let's look at page 21 of the handout I gave you. It is a page from Orelia Ortiz's Nurse's Progress Report. Please read that entry out loud."
" OK. 'After talking to Dr. Morales, I administered the morphine sulfate, Tylenol, Decadron and Valium as prescribed. I reminded Dr. Morales about the G-tube incision. I also mentioned this to Dr. Patterson.' Is that all you want me to read?"
"That will do for a the moment. Is this one of the entries by Orelia Ortiz that you read?"
"I don't recall."
"Well then, since you've testified that you can't read Dr. Morales' handwriting and you don't recall whether you read this entry by Orelia Ortiz, I ask whether you knew Joe Baxter was being given the steroid Decadron?"
"At some point I did."
"When did you know?"
"I don't recall."
"In your medical judgement, was it important for you to know that Joe Baxter was being given rather large doses of Decadron."
Chris Sharp, Patterson's attorney, stood and said, "I object!"
Consuela looked at him, smiled, and said, "OK, since I gave Mr. Urban an objection. I'll give you one. On what basis?"
"On the basis that you're calling it a rather large dose without foundation and secondly, my client did not prescribe it."
"Would you like for me to read the entry in the PDR about dosage amounts for Decadron?"
Chris Sharp said, "Not at this time but I want my objection noted."
Linda Martinez said, "Noted."
Consuela said, "I believe your client will testify that he should have known about the Decadron, if I can continue."
Sharp said, "Note the objection that he did not prescribe it."
Consuela ignored Mr. Sharp and looked at Randy Patterson. "Dr. Patterson, was the Decadron dosage prescribed by Dr. Morales a high dose?"
"I guess so."

"An extremely high dose?"

"Perhaps."

"Was the Decadron prescribed after Joe Baxter became paralyzed?"

"I think so."

"Want to look at the record to be sure?"

"No. It was prescribed after he became paralyzed."

"Was it prescribed after the Vinke brace was placed on Joe Baxter?"

Randy Patterson suddenly began to look miserable. Consuela paused and looked at him. She thought he might just be beginning to understand what had happened.

Consuela looked at him and said, "OK. Look at page 62."

Randy leafed through the pages slowly as if he was trying to give himself time to think. Finally, he said, "OK. I've got it."

"Tell us what that page indicates."

"That the Vinke brace was placed on Joe Baxter."

"And what is the date of that entry?"

"July 8."

"And when was the Decadron started?"

Randy turned the pages back to the entry by Orelia Ortiz. "Hmm...it was July 8."

"Same day, right?"

"Yes."

Consuela put down the folder she was holding. She looked at Randy Patterson. She waited a minute to ask the question, letting him stew a bit. She glanced around the table. The attorneys looked a bit uncomfortable but OK. The doctors were starting to look a bit upset.

"Now, Dr. Patterson. Was the G-tube still in place?"

He answered softly, "Yes." He looked at his attorney Chris Sharp, pleading with his eyes.

Sharp said, "Miss Travis, I know you don't have to grant this but I would like to have a fifteen minute break."

Consuela thought for a minute and decided the break would be helpful to her case because she was sure Randy Patterson would tell Chris Sharp the effect Decadron would have had on the G-tube incision. The sooner the other doctors and lawyers understood what had happened the better, she thought.

"I'll grant a fifteen minute break," she said.

There was shuffling at the table and they all stood. Consuela went to the court reporter and asked if she could get her something to drink.

"Would it be possible to get a small glass of iced tea?" answered Linda Martinez.

Consuela left the conference room and walked over to Marge Kern. "How's it going?" asked Marge.

"I'm pleased. Please fix Linda Martinez a glass of iced tea, OK?"

"Sure. Your dad has called twice," said Marge, smiling.

Consuela looked around and saw no one else had left the conference room. She picked up the phone and called her dad. When he answered, Consuela said, "We were right. The attorneys have only their client's part of the record. Except Walt Urban who had Francisco Catron's full record but I'm even more certain he hasn't studied it. And I think some of the doctors are beginning to catch on."

"Have you finished for the day?"

"No. I'm not finished with Patterson. I'll go for a while longer. Make them squirm a bit. Then I'll do Paul Morales."

"Keep up the good work!"

"I'll try."

Consuela stood by Marge's desk for several minutes, thinking. She went back into the conference room and saw Randy Patterson in deep conversation with his attorney, Chris Sharp. Judy Martin was talking to Walt Urban. She didn't look happy.

Consuela wanted to let Randy Patterson know she understood what had happened without going into too much detail. She'd hold some points for tomorrow when she deposed Sam Boswell.

Consuela tapped the table with a pen and said, "If I can have your attention. Let's get started again." There was some shuffling and Randy Patterson sat back down in the chair by the court reporter.

"Let the record show we've had a fifteen minute break," Consuela said.

"So noted," said Linda Martinez.

"Dr. Patterson. Is the upper stomach normally filled with candida?" said Consuela.

Dr. Patterson looked pained and muttered, "I guess so."

"You guess so? You don't know for sure? Dr. Patterson, isn't it true that candida is usually present in the upper stomach?"

"Yes, that area is usually filled with candida."

"Where was the G-tube placed?"

"Upper stomach."

"Once the Vinke brace was attached to Joe Baxter, did you check the G-tube?"

"Of course."

"Was it still used to feed Joe Baxter?"

"Yes."

"How far down did the bottom of the Vinke brace come."

Chris Sharp said, "Objection!"

Consuela smiled and said, "You're pushing your luck, Mr Sharp. Not this time. I'm not asking how the Vinke brace is put on a patient. I am asking if it came down to the G-tube which this doctor did place."

Consuela paused for a moment. This sudden rush of attempted objections, when the earlier questioning drew almost no response, re-enforced her growing belief that Randy Patterson finally did understand what happened and during the break he had told his attorney. She wondered if any of the other doctors understood and had conferred with their attorneys during the break. She believed that the attorneys arrived at the deposition thinking the whole thing was bogus, that the doctors had acted heroically in trying to save Joe Baxter's life and that this was all just a crass way for the widow to make money.

"Dr Patterson, how far down did the Vinke brace come?"

"I'm not sure."

"Below the chest?"

"Maybe."

"Dr. Patterson, did it cover the top of the G-tube incision?"

Randy Patterson said softly, "It might have."

"Surely you know whether it covered it or not. You just told us you checked the G-tube after the Vinke brace was placed."

Sharp said, " He did not place the Vinke brace! You are badgering the witness."

Consuela answered with a firm voice, "I did not say nor did I suggest he placed the Vinke brace on Joe Baxter. I am asking if it covered the top of the G-tube incision, an incision he created."

Consuela looked at Randy Patterson. She felt sorry for him in some ways. It was Sam Boswell who should have been overseeing Joe's care. Patterson was going to work with these doctors in the future and might need letters of recommendation. She was putting him on the spot.

"Did the Vinke brace cover the top of the G-tube incision?"

"It did," he answered softly. The doctors in the room began to look unhappy. Their attorneys glanced at the doctors and sensed something was wrong.

CHAPTER FIVE

"Dr. Patterson, does the steroid Decadron inhibit the healing of infections, specifically candida related fungal infections?"

"Yes," giving up any pretense of fighting her questions. Randy Patterson finally understood what had happened. He'd been so busy with dozens of patients at the time he'd never had time to put together what had happened.

"Did you ever check the top of the G-tube incision once the Vinke brace was put on Joe Baxter."

"Not until the brace was removed."

"And what did you discover?"

"What do you mean?"

"What was the condition of the tissue at the top of the G-tube incision?"

"Not good."

"What does the term 'necrotic tissue' mean?" Consuela asked, looking at Randy as he lowered his head.

"Dead tissue."

"Do infections cause necrotic tissue?"

"Yes."

Consuela realized that Randy Patterson finally understood and she counted on him to explain it to the lawyers. I'll let this go for now she decided.

"Let me move to a new subject, Dr. Patterson."

Randy looked relieved. He shifted in the seat and said, "OK."

Consuela looked at him and said, "Who was the Admitting Physician on Joe Baxter's case and thus the doctor in overall charge of his care?"

"I don't remember. Either Dr. Boswell or Dr. Roberts."

"Look at page one of the exhibit I gave you. See that imprint on the top of the page? Who does that say was the Admitting Doctor?"

Randy looked at the top of the page and said, "Dr. Sam Boswell."

"What does it mean to be the Admitting Doctor?"

"You're in overall charge of the patient's care."

"Would you say that was an important position if there are several doctors treating the same patient?"

Randy shifted in his chair and said, "I guess so."

"You guess so?"

Walt Urban said, "I object."

Consuela looked at him and out of curiosity decided to hear what his objection was and said, "On what basis?"

"Asked and answered," replied Urban.

Consuela said, "Dr. Patterson said, 'I guess' and I want to know if he knows the answer without guessing."

Consuela looked again at Randy Patterson and said, "Dr. Patterson, is the position of Admitting Doctor especially important in a case with several doctors?"

Randy looked down and said, "Yes."

"Is it especially important when the doctors come from different medical specialities?"

"Yes."

"Why is it especially important in that kind of case?"

"I guess to be sure the treatments work together."

"You guess?"

Walt Urban shouted, "Objection?"

Consuela smiled, looked at him and said, "Are you now representing Randy Patterson?"

"No but I will object in a deposition when I think a question is inappropriate. If we go to trial the judge will rule and you won't be able to ask such a question!"

Consuela looked at Walt Urban and said, "<u>When</u> we go to trial I'm sure the judge will allow me to ask that question. In fact, Mr. Urban, as you well know, we can call the judge right now and ask him if you're allowed to raise such an objection and you know very well that he will tell you that you can't raise such objections."

Consuela stared at Walt Urban. He stared back. Finally, he shrugged his shoulders, acknowledging she was right.

Consuela looked at Randy Patterson and said, "When there are doctors from different specialities working on the same patient, what is the importance of the Admitting Doctor?"

"To be sure the treatments work together."

"Thank you, " said Consuela.

Then she looked at Randy Patterson and said, "Let's look at the notes Dr. Boswell, the Admitting Doctor and thus the doctor in charge of the overall treatment of Joe Baxter, wrote in this case. I'm going to give you the full medical record and I ask that you look at that and not the shorter version we have been using."

"Objection!" shouted Chris Sharp.

"You know I don't have to respond to objections in a deposition. But, I'm curious, what is the basis of your objection?" answered Consuela.

Chapter Five

"My client was not the Admitting Doctor and cannot answer questions that should be directed to the Admitting Doctor."

"I have not yet asked a question about Dr. Boswell's entry. I just asked him to look at the first entry of Dr. Boswell's."

"Miss Martinez, did you get the objection and basis and response?"

Linda Martinez said, "Yes."

Consuela laid the record in front of Randy Patterson and said, "Let's start with page one. Page through and read us the first entry that Dr. Boswell wrote."

Randy Patterson looked at the first page, then turned the page. He looked at the next and the next. He continued turning pages, a look of puzzlement began to show on his face. Finally he looked up and said, "OK. I've found it."

Consuela looked at Randy Patterson and said, "What is the date of that entry?"

Patterson looked down at the medical record and said, "Hmm...July 8."

"Now Dr. Patterson, look at the first page of the medical record. What is the date on that first entry?"

As he turned back to page one, Consuela saw Dr. Boswell trying to get Walt Urban's attention. Urban saw him and looked at him. Boswell signaled he had to talk to him. Urban stood and said, "Could we have a five minute break."

Consuela said, "We're almost done."

Boswell frowned at Urban and shook his head. Urban said, "Sorry, we need a break right now. If you'd be so kind as to allow it."

Consuela said, "Sure. Five minutes."

The attorneys shook their heads.

Linda Martinez stopped typing and stretched her fingers. Consuela watched as Urban and Boswell went to the back of the conference room. Boswell started whispering to Urban. Some of the other attorneys watched and some talked to their clients. Urban began to look concerned. He walked back to the table and glanced at the first page of the medical record, then walked back to Sam Boswell.

Consuela believed he looked at the medical record to check the date Joe Baxter had been admitted to the hospital. She knew he'd seen the date was June 24. Since Urban had just heard that Boswell's first entry wasn't written until July 8, he now realized that his client hadn't written in the Doctors Progress Report for two weeks. He was the doctor in charge and he hadn't written an entry for two weeks.

Consuela prayed that her tactics of the early depositions to avoid revealing Dr. Landis's conclusions, her giving all the attorneys a copy of substantial parts of the record, allowing some objections and breaks, would result in the doctors and lawyers understanding the case and be eager to settle and not go to trial.

After the full five minutes had passed, Consuela tapped a pen on the table and said, "The five minutes are up. Let us continue."

Urban and Boswell sat down and Linda Martinez nodded that she was ready.

"Let the record show that we have had a five minute break at the request of Mr. Urban."

"So noted," said Linda Martinez.

Consuela looked at Randy Patterson and said, "Before the break you found that the first entry by Dr. Boswell in the Doctors Progress Report was dated July 8. I asked you to look at the record and tell us when Joe Baxter was admitted. Tell us that date."

"June 24."

"Was that the date you assisted Dr. Boswell in the initial surgery?"

"Yes."

"Do hospital regulations require that you write an entry in the Doctors Progress Report when you have examined a patient?"

"I believe they do."

"Alright. I am going to move now to one final area about which I want to question you. Were you aware that Joe Baxter complained about numbness and had a weak bi-lateral hand grasp almost from the beginning of his hospitalization?"

"I don't remember when I became aware of that."

"Were you aware that the initial X-rays showed the cervical spine only down to C-5."

"Objection!" said Walt Urban who also represented Simon Webster, the head of radiology.

"I'll humor you. Basis?"

"Not his area of expertise."

"I am only asking if he became aware of the fact. Were you aware that the initial X-ray showed only to C-5?"

"At some point I became aware of that but that wasn't my area of expertise. Those issues were the responsibility of Drs. Roberts and Morales."

"Did Joe Baxter have a cut on his forehead from the accident?"

"I don't remember."

"Please look at the report you wrote after the initial surgery. Page three in the exhibit."

Patterson opened the handout and turned to page three and read it. Then he looked up and said, "Yes, he did."

"Is that why the X-ray of the cervical spine was made at the time of admission?"

"Objection!" shouted Judy Martin and Jorge Lopez. Consuela had been waiting for them to object as they represented the orthopedic surgeons Drs. Morales and Roberts.

Consuela thought she knew what their objection was and her response could help her tomorrow. "OK. I'll let you have a bite of the apple too. Basis?" asked Consuela.

"That is not an area of his expertise," answered Judy Martin.

Consuela looked at them and said, "OK. I'll save that for tomorrow when I depose Drs. Roberts and Morales. Dr. Patterson did you do any emergency room work when you were an intern?"

"Yes."

"Do you remember the criteria used to determine when a hard collar, rather than a soft collar, should be placed around a person's neck who had been in an car wreck?"

"Objection!" shouted Judy Martin and Jorge Lopez.

"Sorry. No more objections." Consuela looked at them and said, "I think any doctor in an emergency room could answer that but I'll let it go. We'll come back to that tomorrow."

Consuela hoped she had planted the idea that she knew a great deal about the mistakes the orthopods had made, enough for them and their lawyers to study the record overnight and during the day tomorrow with their clients. She was convinced that they had not done so. She believed that when they did there was a real chance they would offer to settle as they would want to avoid a public trial.

Consuela looked at Randy Patterson and said, "Dr. Patterson, that is all for now."

Patterson got up from the witness chair and went to his seat.

Consuela said, "I now call Dr. Morales."

Dr. Morales walked to the chair and sat down. Linda Martinez administered the oath.

Consuela looked at him and said, "Dr. Morales, I'm not going to deal with the issue of your handwriting at this time except to ask you if you know that it is difficult to read ."

Morales smiled slightly and said, "So I have been told."

"What are the conditions under which you place a hard collar on a patient?"

"I'm not sure what you mean."

"Dr. Morales surely you know the conditions under which you should use a hard collar to prevent a patient from turning his head."

"If you suspect there may be a fracture of the cervical vertebrae."

"And why might you suspect there might be a fracture?"

"There are many reasons."

"How about an auto accident?"

"Perhaps."

"What if there is a cut on the forehead?"

"Not necessarily."

"A cut on the forehead during a highway accident?"

"Perhaps."

"Would you want an X-Ray of the cervical spine in that circumstance?"

"Yes."

"How many vertebrae should a cervical spine X-Ray show?"

"Depends."

"Are you saying there isn't a standard number of vertebrae that an X-Ray of the cervical spine should show?"

"Depends."

"Depends? Dr. Morales is it your testimony that the standard textbooks on orthopedics are wrong in saying the X-Ray should show the full cervical spine, from C-1 to C-7?"

"No. That is correct."

" I do realize that it isn't your job to take the X-Rays. But isn't it your job to read the X-Rays with the radiologist?"

"I suppose so."

"Would you set a broken leg without looking at the X-Rays?"

"No."

"Why did you place a soft collar on Joe Baxter several days after he was admitted?"

"He complained of some numbness. It was just a precautionary thing. I was most worried about his leg and foot and trying to save them. His left leg was horribly mangled."

"Back to the soft collar. Was it just numbness he complained about or was there something else?"

"I don't remember."

"OK. Please look at page 9 of the exhibit I gave you."

Morales and Judy Martin quickly thumbed to that page. It was a page of notes by Orelia Ortiz. As soon as she saw it, Judy Martin said, "Objection!"

Consuela looked at her, smiled and said, "Basis?"

"These are not his notes."

"No, they are the notes of Orelia Ortiz whose handwriting we can read and they refer to a conversation she had with Dr. Morales. Dr. Morales these notes say that Orelia Ortiz talked to you about numbness and a weak bi-lateral hand grip. Did she talk to you about that?"

Judy Martin looked at Paul Morales and said, "I advise you not to answer that question. Those are not his notes."

Morales looked confused and nodded his head.

"In that case," Consuela said, "we will have to call the judge. Will you come with me Miss Martin and we'll go call the judge." Consuela stood and motioned for Judy Martin to follow her. Judy Martin stood and then shook her head. "Oh, never mind."

Consuela was pleased. Calling the judge during a deposition was sure to irritate the judge. Raising objections and instructing clients not to answer questions during a deposition was almost never allowed and she knew the judge would side with her. So did Judy Martin.

"Miss Martinez did you get the exchange Judy Martin and I just had?"

"Yes."

Consuela said, "Dr. Morales the record will indicate that after several such conversations with Orelia Ortiz, you put a soft collar on Joe Baxter's neck. Isn't that correct?"

"I suppose."

Consuela said, "Dr. Morales, can you turn your head in a soft collar?"

He looked at Judy Martin. She said nothing. He answered, "Yes. Slightly."

"Can you turn your head in a hard collar?"

Again he looked at Judy Martin. She said nothing. He answered, "No."

"Now Dr. Morales, let me see if I have this right. Joe Baxter is brought to the emergency room after a wreck. The paramedics placed a soft collar around his neck because he had a gash on his forehead. The X-Rays show only to C-5. After the surgery he complains of numbness and had a weak bi-lateral hand grasp. You finally put him in a soft collar and order another X-ray. That too only shows down to C-5, you don't put him in a hard collar and you don't order another X-Ray. Is that correct?"

Paul Morales looked miserable and said, "Yes."

Consuela said, "Why didn't you put him in a hard collar?"

Morales answered, "I didn't think he needed it."

Consuela said, "Well, we know what happened."

Martin shouted, "Objection. Improper commentary by Miss Travis."

"Want to go call the judge?"

Judy Martin just stared at her.

Consuela looked down briefly at her notes and then said, "Dr. Morales why did Joe Baxter become paralyzed?"

Morales hesitated and then said, " He had a displaced fracture in his neck."

"And how did he displace the fracture?"

Morales looked down and said, "He turned his head."

"And which vertebrae was fractured and displaced?"

"C-6."

"And it was displaced over which vertebrae?"

"C-7."

"And which vertebrae weren't visible in the only X-Rays of the cervical spine you had before he became paralyzed?"

Morales shifted in the chair. He looked at Judy Martin. She just looked at him since she knew she couldn't object to this question. He finally said, "C-6 and C-7."

"Alright. Let's talk about the Vinke brace. Why did you put Joe in the Vinke brace?"

"Because we were trying to see if we could stabilize him and reduce the swelling. See if feeling returned. We hoped the paralysis was only temporary."

"Is that why you prescribed the Decadron? To reduce the swelling?"

"Of course."

"The Decadron dosage was high, wasn't it?"

"I guess so."

"Want to read the entry from the PDR about dosage?"

"No. It was a high dose. We were desperate to help Joe Baxter."

"When you and Dr. Roberts placed the Vinke brace on Joe, did you observe the G-tube?"

"I really don't remember. That was Dr. Patterson's area."

"Did you consider what the high dose of Decadron would do to that incision?"

"I presumed the surgeons were watching that."

"Are you saying you didn't watch to see what effect the high dosage of Decadron would do to that incision?"

"It was their area."

Consuela paused for a minute and looked at her notes. She could ask more questions but she didn't think she need to. She looked up and said, "That will be all for today. We will begin tomorrow at 4:00 and I may need three or four hours. Thank you."

Linda Martinez looked around the table and said, "This deposition is concluded for the day."

When Consuela got home that night she was tired but in good spirits. She thought the depositions had gone well. She hoped the doctors and lawyers were beginning to see what had happened. She called Margaret and gave her a brief summary of the depositions. She talked to her father for a few minutes.

Fred had brought food home from Jaxon's that he knew Consuela liked. He heated the potato and green chile soup and put the fresh tortilla strips on top. She felt herself relaxing as she spooned the soup, taking time to savor the flavor. Then he said, "And I also got another of your favorites."

He served the two plates of chipolte tostada chips that were topped with pesto-grilled shrimp and fresh guacamole. Consuela smiled and said, "Oh Fred! You know how much I love this. Thank you, sweetheart!"

"You're welcome. And, dear lady, I am now going to fill the Jacuzi so you can really rest and relax."

As she soaked, Consuela thanked God again for Fred. She thought about the depositions and knew she was having an easier time tonight than the doctors and lawyers.

She got to the office before nine o'clock and, after a chat with her father, she studied her notes and planned her strategy. Her phone buzzed and she lifted the receiver. Marge said, "It's Walter Urban on the phone. Want to talk to him?"

"Sure," she said and punched the button. "Good Morning, Mr. Urban."

"Miss Travis, our side talked briefly last night and I am authorized to make a settlement offer so we can end this."

"What is the amount?"

"We are going to offer a generous amount even though we don't think you have much of a case but my clients are busy and don't really have time for all this."

"And the amount?"

"Two hundred thousand."

Consuela laughed and said, "Two hundred thousand? Fine, I'll tell Margaret Baxter about your offer and I'll advise her not to take it and I can pretty much guarantee she won't. Are you at your office? I'll call her and get back to you. Shouldn't take more than a couple of minutes."

"OK." he said.

Consuela called Margaret and told her about the offer.

"That's ridiculous!" Margaret said.

"Exactly my feeling. I think Walt Urban is just trying to feel us out, see if they can get out of this cheaply."

"Well, tell them that Margaret Baxter said, 'Hell no!' And I want to be quoted exactly!"

"I'll quote you exactly. I'll talk to you later."

Consuela called Walt Urban back and gave him Margaret's answer and said, "I'll see you at four."

At four o'clock, attorneys Walt Urban, Judy Martin, Jose Lopez and Chris Sharp were seated around the table. Doctors Sam Boswell, Simon Webster and Don Roberts were seated and they were joined by Francisco Catron, the hospital administrator. Dr. Patterson and Dr. Morales were not present.

Consuela nodded at Linda Martinez and said, " It is four o'clock and we are ready to begin." She said the names of those present so Martinez could make the record.

"I call Simon Webster to be deposed," Consuela said.

Webster moved to the chair by Linda Martinez. She administered the oath and turned to Consuela.

"Dr. Webster, what is your position at Memorial Hospital?"

"I am chief of radiology."

"How long have you held that position?"
" For the past twelve years."
"Are you a member of the American College of Radiology?"
"Yes."
"Do they have a standard for the number of cervical vertebrae that should be visible in an X-ray of the cervical spine?"
"Yes."
"And what is that number?"
"From C-1 to C-7."
"And what did the initial X-ray of Joe Baxter's cervical spine show?"
"From C-1 to C-5."
"Not C-6 and C-7?"
"That is correct."
"Why didn't it show down to C-7?"
"Because of Joe Baxter's very muscular upper body."

Consuela was pleased at how honestly and quickly Simon Webster was answering her questions.

She then asked, "Isn't it the case that with men of muscular upper bodies it is often difficult to X-ray down to C-7?"
"Yes indeed."
"And are there articles in the publications of the American College of Radiology about that difficulty?"
"Indeed there are."
"And when that happens, what do you do?"
"I advise the orthopedic doctors that we should try again so we can picture down to C-7."
"And is that what you did in this case?"
"Indeed I did."
"And did Drs. Morales and Roberts follow your advice?"
"No."

Consuela was pleased with Simon Webster. She made a quick decision and said, "Dr. Webster, that is all and I want to announce that you will be dropped from this suit and I will inform the court of that fact today. Thank you."

Walt Urban smiled and shook Webster's hand when he returned to his seat and picked up his coat and left the room.

Consuela decided to call Francisco Catron next. That would take little time and then she would move to the Big Enchilada, Sam Boswell. She didn't intend to call Don Roberts as she had covered that ground yesterday with Paul Morales, but she wanted Roberts to stew.

"I call Francisco Catron."

Catron got up and went to the chair. Linda Martinez administered the oath and nodded to Consuela.

"Good Afternoon, Mr Catron."

"Good Afternoon."

"What is your position at Memorial Hospital?"

"I am the chief administrator of the hospital."

"Is the hospital a member of the American Hospital Association?"

"Yes."

"And is the hospital accredited by the Joint Commission on Accreditation of Healthcare Organizations?"

"Yes."

" Do the standards for accreditation cover the Doctor's Progress Report?"

"Yes."

"And what do those standards require?"

"That each time a doctor sees a patient in the hospital he or she write an entry and he or she must list all tests ordered, all treatments performed, all medications they administer or ask to have administered."

"So it would be against accreditation standards for a doctor to see a patient and not write an entry?"

"Yes."

"What does it mean when someone is listed as the Admitting Doctor?"

"They have overall responsibility for the patient's care."

"How is it determined who is the doctor in charge."

"Usually the admitting doctor is the doctor in charge. There are occasions when that changes, but certain procedures must be followed in making such a change."

"Were any such procedures to change the doctor in charge followed in this case?"

"Not as far as I know."

"What do the accreditation standards require as to writing the Patient Discharge Note?"

"That it be written promptly."

"Would two weeks be prompt enough?"

"Yes."

"What about six weeks?"

"Six weeks after a patient had been discharged?"
Consuela said, "Yes."
"Much too long, according to the standards."
"Is such a discharge note written when a patient dies at Memorial Hospital?"
"Yes."
"Same time frame?"
"Yes."
"Is it among your duties to see that the procedures we've discussed are followed?"
"Each department is responsible for checking such things and they report to me about such administrative requirements. Of the matters we've discussed, I was ultimately responsible."

Consuela looked at her notes and decided she had elicited all she really needed to at this point. If they went to trial, she could do more. "That will be all for now, Mr. Catron," she said.

Catron stood and looked at Walt Urban. He went to his chair and sat down.

She shuffled her notes and then said, "I call Dr. Sam Boswell."

He looked surprised, thinking she would call Dr. Roberts first. He stood and went to the chair. Linda Martinez gave him the oath and then turned to face Consuela..

"Dr. Boswell, when did you go to Texas A&M?" Consuela asked.

A puzzled look flashed across Boswell's face and he said, "I did not go to Texas A&M! I went to Rice and graduated in 1960."

Consuela pretended to look puzzled and said, "Oh, then when did you become friends with Joe Baxer?"

"I was not a friend of Joe Baxter's."

"You weren't?"

"No. I never met the man until he was admitted to the hospital."

Consuela looked at him and said, "Well, now I am confused. You never sent the Baxter's a bill so I assumed you were friends."

Sam Boswell's face looked stunned. He turned red. Walt Urban looked equally shocked. "Bingo," thought Consuela. She was certain he had forgotten that he had never told his office that Joe Baxter was a patient because he had forgotten he was a patient. She believed he had been thinking he could wiggle out of the fact he had written few notes by saying he talked to Randy Patterson and told him to write the notes. Now, she thought, he was in a trap.

"Do you often do surgery in emergency cases and never send a bill?" Consuela asked.

"Sometimes," he muttered.

"For people you don't know?"

"Sometimes I do so for charity cases."

"Did you think Joe Baxter was a charity case?"

Boswell shuffled his feet and looked down. He was trapped and knew it. He muttered, "I don't remember."

"You don't remember?" asked Consuela. "Dr. Boswell, what criteria do you use when deciding that a patient will be a charity patient," asked Consuela.

"Uh...there are various criteria."

"Tell us what those criteria are."

"Well...when some local charity asks me to do so."

"Did some local charity ask you to take Joe Baxter as a charity patient?"

"I don't recall."

"Do you take a patient as a charity case when they have full medical insurance?"

" Not usually."

"Did you know that Joe Baxter was covered by a medical insurance plan?"

Boswell begin to fidget in his seat and looked at Walt Urban. Urban said, "Objection."

"I really want to hear the basis for this objection so I'm going to allow it. Basis?" answered Consuela

"Badgering the witness," mumbled Urban.

Consuela had to stifle a laugh. She just looked at Urban and said, "I'll try to be really polite in asking the question. Miss Martinez, did you get all that?"

"Objection noted, basis noted," said Linda Martinez.

Consuela looked at Sam Boswell and said, "Dr. Boswell, would you like to see a copy of Joe Baxter's medical insurance plan? And I'm very sorry I didn't include it in the package of material I gave you, but I do have it right here." Consuela reached for a large folder and started looking for the document.

"No. Never mind. I guess he had insurance." said Boswell.

"He did. So let's get back to why you decide to take someone as a charity case. Do you still think you took him as a charity case?"

Chapter Five

"I might have."

"When you do accept a charity case, I presume your office keeps a record of your expenses so that you can claim a tax deduction. Correct?"

Boswell was trapped and he knew it. He finally realized he had never told his office that Joe Baxter was a patient. He looked at Walt Urban and said, " I need a fifteen minute break."

Consuela said, "Your attorney will tell you I don't have to grant a break but I will, just to show I'm not badgering you," Consuela said, smiling at Walt Urban. She then looked at Linda Martinez and nodded her head.

"Note there will be a fifteen minute break," said Martinez.

As Consuela left the room she looked back and saw all the parties go to the back of the room. They were soon involved in a heated discussion. Boswell said little. Consuela walked out and went to Marge Kern's desk.

"How's it going?"

"Really great. I think they know they're in trouble."

"Go girl!" said Marge.

Consuela looked through some mail as she stood there. She wanted to appear unconcerned, ready to resume. At the end of the fifteen minutes, Consuela went back into the conference room.

Judy Martin looked over at her and said, "Miss Travis, we need a few more minutes. We are going to offer you a substantial settlement."

Consuela saw the pained look on Walt Urban's face. Sam Boswell was looking at the floor. The other attorneys were nodding in agreement as were Francisco Catron and Dr. Dan Roberts.

"Fine. I'll be in my office. You can tell Marge Kern when you are ready to talk."

She left the room and walked out to Marge. "Bingo!" she said quietly, "They say they are going to offer a substantial settlement." Marge tried to hide her excitement and just nodded her head. Consuela walked over to her office and went in and sat in a chair that faced the large window. Lights were beginning to come on across the city and the mountain was a dark shape across the sky. She saw an airplane, with wing lights flashing, sinking lower as it prepared to land. "God," she prayed, "Let their offer be one that we can accept, one that is fair to Margaret."

She heard a knock on the door. She stood and went to the door and opened it. Marge was standing there, smiling and said, "They're ready for you."

Consuela walked back into the conference room. Chris Sharp, who had represented Randy Patterson, waited for her to be seated, then said, "Miss Travis, on behalf of all the defendants, we offer one million dollars to settle this case."

Consuela looked at him and said, "Before I call Margaret Baxter, I want you to know that this will be the last offer we will consider. I'll give you five more minutes. If Mrs. Baxter refuses your offer, we'll see you at trial. There will be no individual settlements. You will all agree or there is no settlement. Mrs. Baxter is aware that Texas law would allow a settlement of three million three hundred and fifty thousand dollars."

Judy Martin, turned and looked at the defendants and lawyers. "I told you it wouldn't work. Can I tell her what we are really willing to offer?" Consuela watched as one by one they shook their heads "yes." Walt Urban nodded "yes" vigorously.

"Miss Travis. We have talked to the doctors insurance companies and we are authorized to offer a settlement for the full amount allowed under the law, the amount you just mentioned. Will you please relay that to your client."

"I would be happy to do that right now and I will recommend she accept the settlement." Consuela left the room and went to Marge Kern's desk. "Get Margaret Baxter on the phone. They're offering the full amount!" Marge grinned and dialed the number.

Consuela went into her office and picked up the phone when Marge buzzed. "Hi, Margaret. They have just offered to settle the case for the full three million three hundred and fifty thousand dollars. I recommend you accept. What do you think?"

Margaret started crying and said, "Thank God this is over. Of course, I accept. Do I have to sign documents?"

"Yes, those will be drawn up in the next couple of days. I'll go tell them now."

"Consuela, thank you. You have been so good to me and for me."

"My pleasure."

Consuela went back to the conference room and said, "She accepts."

Chapter Six
A New Beginning

Consuela awoke slowly. She opened her eyes and glanced around the room. Fred was asleep next to her. She stretched and decided to get up and make coffee. Fred stirred and said, "Good morning, Mrs. Cunningham."

Consuela grinned and said, "Good morning, Dr. Cunningham. I'm going to go fix coffee." Consuela put on her robe and went to the kitchen. She looked out the window at the beautiful hills of Tuscany. She fixed the coffee and went out to sit under the pergola and enjoy the view. The Chianti hills toward Siena were beautiful in the early morning light and she could see the high peaks of Monte Amiata beyond. In the distance, she saw two villas sitting atop a small mountain, their yellow walls rising to the red tile roofs.

Fred had done a spectacular job of finding the perfect spot for their honeymoon. They had rented a villa at Borgo San Felice, a fine classic hotel run by the Hotel Relais group. Near the hotel was this villa, sitting alone on the top of a small hill and surrounded by olive trees and the vineyard. The villa had a beautiful living room with a fireplace, a dining room, a kitchen that was fully equipped, a master bedroom and bath and two other smaller bedrooms and baths. Fred had rented it even though it was much bigger than they needed because the privacy was worth the cost. They had a private pergola with table and chairs outside and a private swimming pool.

This was their third morning at San Felice and Consuela finally felt rested from the wedding and the flight to Florence. They had rented a car, managed to make their way out of Florence onto the autostrada, and the drive to San Felice was beautiful.

They had slept most of the first day and had driven to Castelnuovo Berardenga in the afternoon to get some groceries. They loved the fresh produce, the rustic bread loves, the smell of fresh roasted coffee, the wonderful prosciutto. They had bought a bottle of Chianti and the clerk, who spoke beautiful English, had helped them select a "gallo nero", explaining that the sign of gallo nero was a black rooster on the label and that meant it was aged at least four years. When he saw they had prosciutto, he also recommended Vernaccia di San Gimignano, a white wine that he said was especially good with prosciutto. Their meal that night was simple: proscuitto and figs, rustic bread dipped in extra virgin olive oil and herbs, and the white wine. They agreed that the clerk at the supermarket knew his stuff.

Their second day was spent walking around the grounds of the Borgo San Felice and spending time together, enjoying the love they felt. They ate lunch at their villa and dinner at Poggio Antico, the restaurant at the hotel. They spent several hours under the pergola, remembering their wedding.

Fred told her that night about Sam Boswell. "He came to me at the hospital and said he wanted to talk to me," Fred began. "He then told me that you were right. I told him I knew nothing about the case and he said he understood, but wanted me to know that you had been correct in your judgement about the case, that he was sure you revealed so much at the deposition so they would settle and not have a public trial. He was grateful. He said he had simply forgotten he had Joe Baxter as a patient and that had never happened to him before. He wanted to come to the wedding and talk to Margaret Baxter. I told him that wouldn't be a good idea, so that's why he wasn't there. As you know, the other doctors came."

Consuela had been surprised. All she had told Fred was that there was a settlement. He had been pleased that there wasn't going to be a public trial.

They had talked about how beautiful St. Clement's was the day of the wedding. They agreed that Bill Travis looked terrific in his tux as he walked Consuela down the aisle and that Maria had never been more beautiful. Fred's parents were delighted with the wedding and had long admired and loved Consuela. Cynthia had managed to look beautifully pregnant in her matron-of-honor dress and Jim was a proud and handsome best man. Margaret Baxter had smiled her wonderful, new full smile at Consuela as she came down the aisle.

Fred and Consuela laughed as they remembered the reception at the country club and the private talk they had with the orchestra, telling them no matter what Cynthia said, there was not going to be a conga line.

Fred came out to the pergola and kissed Consuela. She poured him a cup of coffee. "The view is so beautiful. We've got to come back," he said.

"Absolutely and when we have kids, we'll bring them," Consuela said.

Chapter Six

Fred smiled in agreement. "Well, Mrs. Cunningham, today's the day we go to Florence and tour the Uffizi. I'm glad we waited. I feel really rested and I've got energy back."

"Me too. Last night I looked at the handbook that Cynthia gave us with all her notations about what we had to see at the Uffizi. I'm so glad she told us get the tickets on-line so we don't have to wait. It's going to be great. Did that guy at the desk at the hotel give you good directions about taking the train?"

"Yep. We'll drive to Castelnuovo and park the car at the station, buy our tickets and hop aboard."

When they arrived at the train station in Florence they could see the dome of Santa Maria del Fiore, Il Duomo, and started down a street in that direction. When they reached the plaza they stood and looked up at the beautiful walls, in white and green marble, gleaming in the sunlight. Fred took Consuela's hand and they looked at the dome, soaring up into the morning sky. "Brunelleschi's dome. What a wonder!" said Consuela.

They entered the cathedral and looked up into the dome, walked around and finally sat in a pew, knelt and prayed. "Dear God," prayed Consuela, "Thank you for bringing us here. Thank you for Fred, for the gift of our love. Thank you for my life. Thank you for all your creation."

They left the cathedral and walked toward the Uffizi. They were a half-hour early and stopped at an espresso bar and had café latte and a small roll. As they sat at a table next to the sidewalk they enjoyed looking at the people going by. They soon realized there were people from all over the world. Florence, the capital of the Renaissance, was busy and energetic. They could see the Arno River with people walking their dogs on the river bank. The Ponte Vecchio arched over the river.

They followed Cynthia's instructions when they entered the Uffizi and went immediately to see Botticelli's Birth of Venus and Primavera. Fred and Consuela had seen many reproductions of the paintings but they were overwhelmed when they saw the paintings. The depth of the colors, the flow of the images, the sheer beauty was triumphant. They did see work by Giotto and Michelangelo and Carravaggio but nothing remained in their hearts and minds as did the Botticellis.

That night they lay in bed talking. They agreed they would return during the next year. They still had two days and would return to Florence tomorrow to see the statue of David and eat at a restaurant recommended by Jim and Cynthia, but so much was left unexplored. They had been able to arrange for only a one week honeymoon. Fred had to return to his practice and Consuela had cases needing her attention.

Consuela said, "I'm glad the malpractice case is over."

"Me too," said Fred.

"Should I change the name of the law firm to Travis and Cunningham?"

"Doesn't matter to me, sweetheart. I know you're my wife. Travis and Travis is a gold medal name in El Paso."

"It is...but I love my new name. Consuela Travis Cunningham."

"The decision is entirely up to you and your dad."

Consuela drifted off to sleep, snuggled in the arms of the man she loved.

The End

Acknowledgments

This is a work of fiction. I grew up in El Paso but have not lived there since the early 1960's, but during the past year, as I wrote this novel, I felt I was home again. The beauty of the high desert country and the mountains were prominent in my mind's eye; the easy mix of Mexican and American cultures, their food, art, music and language again filled my soul.

I am grateful to my daughter, Kimberly Herard, and my friend, Carole Duncan, for their patience in reading and making suggestions and catching my typos. Their encouragement was vital. I thank my rector, Fr. Frank Cooper, and friends at Christ the King Episcopal Church in Santa Rosa Beach, Florida, including Sandra and Joe Middleton, Cornelia Boone and Catherine Dickson for reading the novel and making suggestions. I am grateful to my friend Liz Smith for sending me so many books to read, books that taught me the value of a good story.

Finally, I thank Google for making it possible to do extended research online!

Barbara Kaster

Author Biography

Barbara Kaster was born in El Paso, Texas, graduated from Texas Western College with Bachelor's and Master's degrees, and taught in the El Paso public schools before receiving her Ph.D. from The University of Texas at Austin. After teaching at three universities, she accepted the position as Harrison King McCann Professor of Communications at Bowdoin College in Brunswick, Maine where she spent the last twenty years of her academic career. She produced and directed six documentary films.

She lives in Destin, Florida with her friend Carole Duncan and has one daughter, Kimberly Herard, wife of Thomas Herard, of Stewart, Mississippi. Barbara is the very proud great-grandmother of Hannah May Herard, daughter of L.B. and Leah Herard.

Barbara is active in her church, Christ the King Episcopal Church in Santa Rosa Beach, Florida.

Made in the USA